Th
V
and other
spinechilling stories

Other titles by Pamela Oldfield

The Mill Pond Ghost and other stories

Adventures on the Santa Lucia series
Secret Persuader
Bomb Alert

Pamela Oldfield

The Haunting of Wayne Briggs and other spinechilling stories

Illustrated by
David Senior

Lions
An Imprint of HarperCollinsPublishers

The Haunting of Wayne Briggs and other spinechilling stories
was first published in Lions in 1993

Lions is an imprint of HarperCollins Children's Division,
part of HarperCollins Publishers Ltd,
77-85 Fulham Palace Road,
Hammersmith, London W6 8JB.

Printed and bound in Great Britain by
HarperCollins Manufacturing, Glasgow

Contents

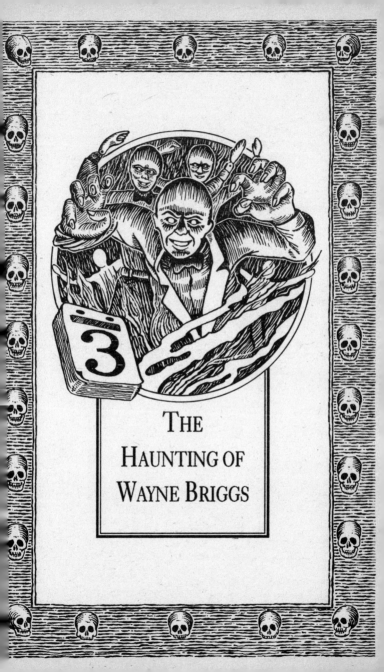

THE
HAUNTING OF
WAYNE BRIGGS

The Haunting of Wayne Briggs

Wayne was smart. Smarter than the rest of his class – and ruthless with it! He prided himself on being tough and on knowing what he wanted out of life. What Wayne wanted was money, but he was too smart to work for it. That was for idiots like Jimmi and Mick. Jimmi delivered papers seven days a week and had to get up at six o'clock every morning. Wayne thought he was "off his rocker" and told him so whenever he got the chance. Mick was just as bad, in Wayne's opinion. He worked at a garage, washing down cars. Every Saturday.

Wayne had decided that the only way to get rich quick was to steal the money, and that's why he had to be smarter than the rest. He'd thought it all out very carefully, and had already put the first part of his plan into action.

Wayne had taken a Saturday job at Dickinson's Department Store. He worked there every morning as a "gopher". That, they had told him, meant being a glorified errand boy. Carrying messages from one department to the other and going to the nearby snack bar to fetch sandwiches in the lunch hour.

"Go fer this and go fer that!" one of the lady assistants had explained with a laugh. "Go-fer. Gopher! Get it?"

Wayne got it, but he thought she was pathetic. They all were. Especially Miss Baybridge. She was the worst, thought Wayne resentfully. She was Mr Dickinson's secretary and thought herself "the bee's knees"! Oh yes! They all thought themselves a cut above him.

He could hear Miss Baybridge's prim voice now as she ordered her sandwiches.

"I want ham and lettuce in brown bread and liver sausage in a bun – and don't forget the coleslaw."

Wayne got it wrong on purpose. He would bring liver sausage in brown bread and luncheon meat in the bun – and no coleslaw. He got them all wrong. They moaned at him week after week, but he didn't care. It was all part of the plan to make them think he was dim. Too dim for part two of his plan, which was to rob the petty cash tin which was kept in the top drawer of the manager's desk.

There was never a chance to get at it during working hours, so Wayne decided to come back one evening when the store was empty. It would be so easy, and on Monday morning when they told him about the theft he would be all surprised. He was looking forward to that.

The big day arrived at last and everyone went home at five thirty as usual. By seven o'clock it was dark as Wayne strolled nonchalantly past the brightly lit windows of the department store, pretending to examine the clothes which the window dummies were wearing. With his hands in his pockets he whistled cheerfully as a police car drifted along the High Street, its blue light reflected in the shop windows.

The police were idiots too, he told himself smugly, but he waited until the car had turned the corner before he nipped smartly down the little alley that ran alongside the store. Round to the back where the lorries unloaded and further still to where he had propped open the toilet window last thing that afternoon. If the elderly caretaker had closed it Wayne's plan would be unworkable, but the old man was an idiot. Sure enough the window was open and, after a quick glance around him, Wayne climbed inside.

He knew the route he must take – nothing had been left to chance. He was too smart for that. Through "Perfumes" and "Ladies' Separates" and then turn right through "Children's Wear" and left past the men's umbrellas. Nervously he moved across the carpeted floor, his ears alerted for any sound that might suggest the store was not empty. A creak in the darkness overhead made him freeze but no, it was nothing. With a sigh of relief he moved on until a distant "clank" stopped him again. Probably the plumbing, he told himself, but he was not enjoying himself as much as he had expected. The empty store was full of shadows and it would be easy to let his imagination run riot.

He made his way along to the stairs (the lifts were switched off at night) and, switching on his pencil-thin torch, made his way up past the hairdresser's glossy photographs and the arrow which pointed customers ever upward in search of the restaurant.

To reach the manager's office he then had to pass through the men's outfitters, and in the gloom the dummies appeared taller and unnaturally thin. Their shiny faces seemed gaunt, almost sinister, and the eyes were watchful. He felt a small shudder of apprehension but dispelled it instantly by saying loudly, "Well, here I am! Any moment now!"

He was annoyed to discover that his voice shook a little. It couldn't be fear so it must be the temperature, he assured himself. It was January, and now that the central heating had been turned off the store was growing chilly. Yes. That was it.

A sudden noise made him halt in his tracks. It sounded like a sigh but he knew that was impossible. He was alone in the store. Wayne was certain that he was imagining things, but his heart beat faster nonetheless.

He leant back against one of the counters and flashed his torch around, just to make sure that his fears were groundless. The thin beam of light lit up one of the dummies, and for a horrible moment he thought the eyes moved!

"Don't be such a twit!" he told himself sternly and continued on his way towards the manager's office where the petty cash tin was kept.

It took no more than a minute to force the lock on the door with the screwdriver he had brought in the back pocket of his jeans. Then he was inside the office and was soon getting to work on the lock of the top drawer. The wood splintered as he wrenched the drawer open, but Wayne was in no mood to worry about trifles.

"Now, Mr Stupid Dickinson!" he muttered. "Let's see how you like this!"

It would serve the old man right, he thought gleefully. Stuck-up fool! Always so smug and always boasting about the firm. Anyone would think it was Harrods, the way he went on about it. Just because Dickinson's had been started by his grandfather.

"Oh boy!"

Wayne whistled appreciatively as he lifted the lid of the metal cash box and saw the roll of banknotes inside. "Very tasty!" he grinned, and already he could see the huge transistor radio he would buy with the money.

Suddenly he froze, his fist clenched round the bundle of notes. There *was* someone else in the store. Someone in menswear! He heard a voice quite distinctly, like an urgent whisper. He couldn't catch what was said, but another voice answered the first. They sounded alarmed. Whoever they were they had obviously seen him!

Wayne looked desperately round for a way out. The windows were double glazed and unopenable, and there was no other door. He would have to make a dash for it.

The voice came more clearly. "Fetch help!" It was a thin voice. An elderly voice. Was it the caretaker? he wondered.

There were more voices.

"Sound the alarm!"

"Get everybody out!"

"Send for the fire engine!"

The fire engine? What on earth were they talking about? he thought irritably. He was robbing the place, not setting fire to it. The thin voices grew sharper, but nobody entered the office and Wayne took the opportunity to hide behind the door. He had seen this trick used in countless movies. As they came in he would dodge past them and make a run for it.

There was a picture hanging on the wall behind him and he suddenly saw that in fact it wasn't a picture at all, but a series of newspaper cuttings that had been framed. One showed quite clearly a large building burning fiercely, and it made the hair on Wayne's neck bristle. A headline stood out in the light of the torch.

FIRE DAMAGES DEPARTMENT STORE

As the voices grew louder, Wayne sensed a growing panic in their voices. Cautiously he peeped round the door and nearly fainted with fright. *The store dummies were talking to each other!* They were!

He blinked his eyes – but there was no disputing the facts. Slowly, clumsily, the dummies moved around as though in slow motion. Then one of them turned towards Wayne – and the nightmare began.

With one cry they moved towards him, their arms outstretched to bar his way.

"He did it!" they cried, their ghostly voices charged with a terrible rage. "Stop him! Catch him! Don't let him get away."

Wayne's limbs felt leaden as he decided to make a dash for it. He dodged this way and that; he tried everything he knew, but wherever he moved the hateful, clutching arms were there to prevent his escape. The glaring lifeless eyes burned into his. Wayne was petrified. He was paralysed with fear as inexorably the half-human figures closed in on him, snatching at his clothes and scratching his face and hands with stiff, cold fingers.

He whimpered "Let me go! Please! Please don't hurt me!" but a smooth hand fastened tightly round his wrist and with a cry of despair Wayne acknowledged that he was lost.

He began to scream, louder and louder, and the sound of his screams mingled with a new sound. The crackle of flames and the clangour of the fire engine was the last thing he remembered before he fainted.

The papers next morning featured a report about a break-in at Dickinson's Department Store.

YOUTH HELD AFTER ROBBERY

was the headline.

Mr Dickinson read the report to his secretary and then shook his head.

"What I don't understand is what prevented his escape," he told her. "He had the money in his pocket but there he was, lying on the floor, out to the world! The hospital reckoned he had fainted, but why should he?"

Miss Baybridge shrugged her shoulders. "Guilty conscience?" she suggested without much conviction.

Mr Dickinson frowned unhappily. "Something happened – but what? Poor Wayne. He was such a foolish sort of boy. A bit slow, if you know what I mean, but quite likable. Who'd have thought he'd do a thing like this? Steal from his employers!"

Miss Baybridge sniffed disapprovingly. "Well, he won't be missed," she said. "He wasn't exactly 'Brain of Britain'! He couldn't even get the orders right for the sandwiches!"

"But what *happened* here?" her employer repeated with a sigh. "There's more to it than meets the eye! And have you noticed something rather odd? Yesterday's date?"

She shook her head.

"It's the anniversary of the fire! The fire that killed my father and two other members of staff. They were trapped in the menswear department and were overcome by smoke."

"A fire? Oo-er!" she said. "I didn't know about that."

"It was before your time, my dear," he assured her. "The third of January, exactly twenty years ago to the day. Now that's what I call a coincidence."

The old man crossed the room to stand beside the framed newspaper cuttings – cuttings which he had read so many times before. He gazed at the faded photograph of his father and pursed his lips.

"I wonder," he said softly. "I wouldn't put it past the old devil. Him and Jones and poor old Mr Blakey. I just wonder . . ."

THE
VAMPIRE

The Vampire

"Two seven three two four?"

"Mrs Bamber, can I speak to Mum, please?"

"Is that you, Emma?"

"Yes. Can I—"

"You can, dear, but we've just sat down to dinner. I'm just serving the soup so if it could wait—"

"It can't wait. *Please*, Mrs Bamber, it's very important!"

"Oh well, if you must. I'll fetch her . . ."

A pause.

"Emma, what is it? Mrs Bamber said it was—"

"Mum, there's something horrible outside my bedroom window! I'm scared! Please come home, Mum."

"Something horrible? Whatever are you talking about? How can *anything* be outside your bedroom window? Your room's upstairs."

"I know. That's why I'm scared. It keeps tapping at the window."

"What does?"

"Whatever it is. I don't know because I'm too

19

scared to look. I'm too scared to pull back the curtains. Oh, I *wish* you'd come home. *Please*, Mum!"

"Look, Emma, I can't just walk out on the dinner party. Poor Lorna's gone to *so* much trouble. It wouldn't be fair. Anyway, I hardly ever go out, and you said yourself that it would do me good. You almost pushed me out of the house!"

"But I'm scared, Mum!"

"It's probably a branch from the pear tree."

"It can't be. Mr Turnbull cut it back less than a month ago. Don't you remember?"

"Oh yes. That's right, love. He did. Well, maybe it's—"

"*Mum!* It's banging on the window now! Really hard. Can't you hear it?"

"No, Emma, I can't. Look, love, go to the window, pull back the curtain and tell me what you see. I'm sure there's nothing there . . . Emma? Do you hear what I say? Go to the window—"

"No! I daren't! I won't!"

"Emma! There's no need for these hysterics. Just tell me calmly."

"No!"

"Then leave the curtains pulled, go downstairs and do your homework in the kitchen. You don't have to work in your room. I simply can't walk out on Lorna just because you imagine there is something horrible—"

"There *is!* I know it!"

"No you don't know it because you won't look. Now take your homework and . . . Emma, are you still there? Lorna says the soup's getting cold and the others have finished theirs so I must go. Listen, I'll ring you as soon as we've finished the meal and – What was that? I thought I heard a voice. Who's there with you? . . . Emma, can you hear me? . . . Emma! . . . *Emma!* . . . Speak to me. What's going on?"

"He wants to come in, Mum."

"What? I can hardly hear you. Who wants to come in?"

"The voice is a man's voice. He says he wants to come in. He's begging me to let him in."

"Don't talk such nonsense! Emma, listen to me. I'm going to put the phone down and ring Mr Carter next door and ask him to come round and make sure there's no one there. Just to put your mind at rest. Do you hear me, Emma? Mr Carter will pop round to . . . what was that? That swishing noise . . .Emma? . . . Emma!"

"It was the curtains, Mum, I was pulling back the curtains."

"Why are you whispering, love? I can hardly hear you."

"I've . . . pulled . . . back . . . the . . . curtains . . ."

"At last. Good girl. And *is* there anything out there?"

"There's a vampire."

"A *what*? I thought you said vampire."

"He wants to come in. He looks so terribly sad. He's begging me to open the window and let him in."

"Now, that's quite enough of that, Emma. You'll only make yourself *more* frightened . . . I must go and have my soup, but I'll ring next door for you first. Do you hear me, Emma? I'm ringing Mr Carter, so when he comes let him in and he'll check around for you. Your grandmother was right. You *do* watch too many horror movies! I'll put the phone down now and ring Mr Carter. Vampires! Really, Emma, you make me cross sometimes. There are no such things as vampires. I can assure you of that. Now, I'm going to hang up and ring Mr Carter."

"Mum, I'm going to let him in."

"You're going to – oh I see. Mr Carter. Yes. And then get on with your homework. Bye for now, love. I'll see you later."

"I'm so terribly sorry, everyone. That was my daughter, Emma. She's so highly strung. She gets herself into such a state. Too imaginative by far! . . . Oh, this soup's delicious. No, it's not cold. No, really, Lorna. It's delicious. I tried to ring our next door neighbour, but he's not answering. I'll try again later, but you know how children are. By the time he gets round there she'll have forgotten all about funny noises and vampires at the window. Probably be watching something ghastly on the telly instead. She's really into horror and sci-fi and all that stuff. Frankenstein and things from outer space and plants that eat people! . . . Ooh! Rack of lamb! What a treat! Lorna, you really are a tremendous cook . . ."

"Is that the police! There's been a – what? My name? Oh. I'm Ron Carter. There's been a dreadful – what's that? My address? What the hell does that matter? I'm trying to tell you there's been a – OK! *OK!* It's twenty seven, Brook Avenue, off Higham High Street . . . No, I don't know the post code. There's been a dreadful accident – or something. Yes, the kid next door . . . A girl. Her mother rang me and – what time? How do I know? Oh, yes I do. It was right at the end of *The Bill.* I went next door after her mother rang and asked me to pop round because Emma, that's the girl, was alone in the house and she was getting herself into a state . . . Into a state? Scared. Frightened. Rambling about vampires and wanting her mother to come home. Her mother's a widow and she was invited out to dinner. Poor woman. She doesn't get out much and she was *so* looking forward to it. You'd have thought she was going to dinner with the Queen! . . .

What? Oh, where was she? About half an hour's drive from here . . . I have a spare key in case they ever get locked out. I went round and found Emma. It gave me quite a shock – you'll need a doctor, Sergeant, or an ambulance or whatever. Poor kid looks terrible. White as a sheet. Whiter, really. Like chalk, I'd say. She was lying on the bed with her eyes shut and the window was open. . . . Yes. Wide open. Swinging to and fro on its hinges. Someone *could* have climbed in, but they'd have needed a ladder. I looked out, but there's not one there at the moment. Unless whoever it was took it with them . . . No, not very likely, I admit . . . No, the poor kid's not said a word. How can she? She's unconscious . . . Well, she might be dead but I thought I could hear her heart beating, but very faintly. What's that? You're on your way? Good. Yes, I'll wait here. I shall have to ring her mother. She doesn't know yet . . . Any sign of a what? A struggle?

No. I don't think so. She looks sort of peaceful. But I did notice something, and it gave me a creepy feeling at the back of my neck. As though my hair was standing on end. What there is of it. I'm not bald exactly but – what? Oh, keep to the point. Sorry. Well, there are these two funny marks on her neck. As though someone had jabbed her with something sharp. Two red marks, side by side, about three inches apart. Like what? *Puncture* marks? I suppose so. Yes . . . No. I've no idea. I mean, what *could* they be? . . . You tell me . . ."

ARIANNA

Arianna

Meg allowed her fingers to hover over the keyboard as she searched her mind for the exact word to describe Arianna's feelings. "Rage" was too strong a word. "Anger" might do. Or "indignation", perhaps? She stared at the screen with narrowed eyes and thought for the hundredth time how much she disliked her heroines. The trouble was that the readers of Meg's books adored them and her publishers were always asking for a novel that would please her readers.

It was so unfair. The heroines were always strikingly beautiful with large hazel eyes, flawless complexions and long graceful limbs. Meg's own eyes were like two dark currants and her face was the colour of overcooked cake. As for her legs and arms – well, she preferred not to think about them. Her present heroine went by the name of Arianna and she was always "opening her eyes wide like a startled fawn". If Meg opened her own eyes wide she looked like a startled rock cake.

"Spoilt little beast!" Meg muttered as she finished the sentence and sat back in her chair.

Oh, how she hated Arianna! This particular heroine was worse than most for she was destined to marry a Greek millionaire and live happily ever after. There were no millionaires in Meg's life. She lived in a small semi-detached house in a quiet suburb of London. A very exclusive area, for Meg wasn't poor, but she wouldn't actually object to a tall, handsome husband with a luxury yacht.

With a sigh she recalled her editor's words.

"You are a teller of fairy tales, Meg. A spinner of fantasies. You give your readers what they want."

Meg knew that was true. She also knew that some of her readers believed that the characters in her books were real people. When one of them died they would send flowers to the publisher! "Humbug!" muttered Meg rebelliously. "I'm sick of all this pretence. Life isn't a bit like a fairy tale. Why shouldn't I tell it how it is?"

She glared at the word processor as though it were somehow responsible. The screen stared back at her, the cursor winking encouragement like the faithful creature it was. Meg half-expected it to wag its tail.

She reached out and patted it.

"I don't blame you," she said. "It's this blasted Arianna!"

Suddenly an idea came to her. An idea so tempting that she gave a little whoop of excitement.

She turned to her scribbled notes to remind herself of the fate she had prepared for Arianna.

Arianna the poor little secretary was going to marry Marcos Kopodopolous, the son of Demetrius Kopodopolous who was a millionaire twice over. She would meet him when his Rolls Royce drove past her at great speed and splashed her with muddy water.

"A *lot* of muddy water!" said Meg bitterly.

He would be on his way to a business meeting in Miami but would stop the car and get out to apologize and would discover that she was a secretary. By an astonishing coincidence his own secretary had just been struck down with flu and Arianna would go instead.

"Poppycock!" Meg snarled.

Eventually Arianna would meet Marcos's sister Eva who was, of course, dark, brooding and beautiful. They would hate each other on sight and Eva would try to part Arianna and Marcos. "But just suppose . . .!" whispered Meg. There was a fierce gleam in her small brown eyes which made her look like a hungry wolf and she drummed podgy fingers on the desk top.

"You are in for a nasty surprise, Arianna!" she muttered.

This time her heroine would "come unstuck".

With a smile Meg glanced at the clock. Time for her bedtime cocoa. Gently she closed down the word processor and made her way to the kitchen.

An hour later she was still sitting at the kitchen table and her plans for Arianna's downfall were complete.

First thing next morning she settled herself at her desk and reached for her pen and began to reframe the story.

1) Eva Kopodopolous would become insanely jealous of Arianna and would plan to kill her.

2) She would buy a gun and lie in wait for her one dark night.

3) In the darkness she would not see that Arianna and Marcos were together and she would shoot her brother by mistake.

Meg sat back in her chair smirking with satisfaction.

"You see what I have in mind for you, Arianna?" she demanded with a chuckle. "You will never marry your rich millionaire now!"

Meg knew that her editor would hate the book and so would her readers, but she was past caring. All she could think about was the revenge she would take on her beautiful heroine. She began to work, her fingers flying over the keys. She was enjoying it so much that she didn't bother to stop for any lunch. Time for her cocoa came and went, and still Meg's inspired fingers stabbed away at the keys. The clock in the hall chimed twelve o'clock. Midnight.

Suddenly Meg stopped typing and clapped her hands with delight.

"Better and better!" she cried. "Instead of Eva shooting her I shall make Marcos do it. Yes, yes! Of course! He has been secretly carrying a gun ever since he was once threatened by an anonymous letter and he doesn't know it's Eva shooting at them and he shoots back—!" She leaped to her feet in her excitement." Better still he shoots both of them! He shoots his beautiful sister *and* his beautiful Arianna! Oh, I like it!"

A voice behind her said, "Oh you do, do you?"

Meg froze. She lived alone.

The voice continued, silvery smooth. "Put your hands up and turn round slowly."

As Meg did so, her mouth fell open in surprise, for Arianna stood just inside the door. Unmistakably Arianna. The same wide hazel eyes; the same graceful limbs.

"Arianna!" Meg stammered. "What are you doing here? I mean, how can you – that is, what are you doing here? And why are you holding a gun?" Her confused mind grappled with the problem. "You've got it wrong," she explained. "It's not you that carries the gun, it's—"

"It's me!"

A tall dark handsome man appeared silently from behind the floor-length curtains that hung at the patio doors. "Glided" might be a better word than "appeared", Meg thought.

"Yes!" Meg said eagerly. "You and—"

"And me!"

By this time Meg was recovering from her shock and the sight of Eva, impeccably dressed in a clinging black gown decorated with rhinestones, did not surprise her.

The three characters stared at Meg and the three pistols did not waver. Meg felt a moment's uneasiness as she returned their stares.

After a long silence she asked, "But what are you doing here?"

Arianna smiled. "We don't like the plot of your latest novel."

Meg said "Ah!" but she still felt reasonably confident that she could handle the situation. After all these were not real people, they were phantoms. Plucked from her own imagination. She thought it likely that she had fallen asleep at her desk and that this was a nightmare.

Eva said, "You don't think we'll do it, do you?"

"Do what?"

"Kill you."

"No, I don't. Why should you? You are my creations, so without me you would cease to exist. I mean, who would finish the story if I were dead?"

"Arianna would." Marcos's voice was deeper than she had expected and his dark eyes were like brown velvet. "She can type. She's a secretary, remember?"

Meg wasn't listening. She was thinking how very attractive he was and could quite see why any heroine would fall in love with him. Even without his millions! Impulsively she tried to flutter her eyelashes the way her heroines did.

Arianna said cruelly, "Something in your eye, dear?" and they all laughed.

Meg felt a deep anger swelling within her (or was it rage?) and stepped forward. "If you think for a moment—" she began, but at that moment Marcos said, "One!"

Eva said, "Two!"

And Arianna said, "Three!"

All three pistols fired at once and Meg fell backwards, clutching at the desk to save herself. A sheaf of papers fluttered around her as she lay spreadeagled on the carpet. Without another word the three characters hurried to the word processor and Arianna sat down in Meg's chair.

They found Meg's body two days later and the doctor said it must have been a heart attack. Her picture was in all the newspapers with an accompanying article listing some of her best-known books. The article went on to say how fortunate it was that just before her death she had completed another heartwarming novel.

A SINISTER
WARNING

A Sinister Warning

The dust was there when he woke up. A thick layer of dust which lay on his bedside table like grey snow. For a moment Colin stared at it in astonishment. It certainly had not been there when he went to bed the night before. Slowly he sat up in bed and then sneezed violently as the dust on his duvet cover was disturbed and went up his nose. With growing astonishment he stared around his room and saw that the dust was everywhere. His bookcase, desk, chair – every flat surface had disappeared under the grey dust. He sat for a moment and then, turning, saw that the dust lay across his pillow, save for the area where his head had been. As he stared around his astonishment gave way to uneasiness. His mother was not the world's best housekeeper, he knew that, and she joked about it often enough, but he had never seen dust as thick as this.

Carefully he slid out of bed and felt for his ancient trainers which he wore about the house instead of slippers. When he found them he wrinkled his nose in disgust as he saw that they, too, were thick with dust. He banged them together to disperse it and then slipped his feet into them. The dust that remained was gritty, not a bit like normal dust.

He walked through the dust to the bedroom door, opened it gingerly, and found to his relief that the hall was apparently clean. He turned left into the kitchen where his mother was reading the paper while she waited for her shredded wheat to soften in the milk. She liked it soggy.

"My room's full of dust," Colin told her. "Not just a bit. Full of dust. Thick dust like snow."

She looked up irritably. "You know where the dusters are kept," she said sharply. "I've told you before. It's your room. You should keep it clean."

"You don't understand," he said. "I mean a funny kind of dust. Strange dust. I mean it, Mum. It's really weird."

She spooned sugar on to her cereal. Colin had told her about calories and about heart disease; he had told her too many times to count, she took no notice at all. She liked things sweet. She took a large mouthful and said, "Delicious!"

Colin's mother could be very irritating at times.

"I think you should see it," Colin told her.

"See what?"

"The dust in my room."

"I've seen dust before," she said. "It's no big deal."

"This dust is different," said Colin. He could see she was in one of her awkward moods. She had been a different person since her husband died. She seemed angry, as though he had died on purpose to make their life difficult. Once, in a fit of despair, she had said that if he had cared about them at all he would never have left them.

Now he said, "Please, Mum! Just come and look," and something in his voice made her agree.

Together they stared at the thick grey dust. Colin's footprints were clearly visible across the carpet.

Colin's mother was visibly shaken by the sight.

"It's uncanny!" she whispered. "It's horrible! Ugh!"

She shuddered and Colin's uneasiness became apprehension. She was right. There was something eerie about it.

"Let's look at the rest of the place," she suggested shakily, but a quick tour of their small flat revealed nothing out of the ordinary.

At last they went back to Colin's room, no wiser than before. "I'll get the hoover out," his mother said. "I'll ring them at work and say I'll be late in. You get off to school."

When Colin returned home late that afternoon his room was gleaming. He grinned as he looked around and smelt the polish. His mother had done a good job. She had even cleaned the silver frame which held the photograph of Colin's father. That was just like Mum, he reflected. She let things slide for ages then went mad! He smiled as he crossed to the window which overlooked the road. He saw her walking along the pavement, talking to one of the neighbours. Probably telling her about the strange dust. She said "Cheerio!" and pushed open the gate which Colin's father had made when the original one finally fell to pieces. In the small front garden she paused to pull some dead flower heads from the Michaelmas daisies.

The evening was like any other evening. Colin cooked corned beef hash, which was one of his specialities, and his mother washed up while he did his homework. Then they watched television and went to bed. Colin had forgotten all about the dust.

But the next morning it was back!

This time he was really scared and without waiting to put on his trainers he rushed out of the room and yelled to his mother, who was in the bathroom, cleaning her teeth. They stood together in the doorway and stared in dismay at the thick grey dust. Seeing that his mother was temporarily lost for words Colin said shakily "All that hoovering for nothing!" and tried to laugh.

After a moment she said "That does it! That really does it!"

Colin knew at once what she meant.

Ever since his father's death they had been asking for a council house because with only one income the rent on their present flat was too high. More than once they had fallen behind with it and the landlord had been very sarcastic. On one occasion he had threatened to throw them out into the street.

Colin's mother looked at him. "I'm going to fetch the man from the council," she said. "He can see what we have to put up with here. They'll have to find us somewhere else."

"Will they?" Colin was dubious.

"Of course they will." His mother bristled indignantly and waved a hand to indicate the dust-laden room. "That room's a health hazard! How can you sleep in a room like that? And where else can you sleep?" She looked at him and he saw that she was talking herself into it.

Colin shrugged. He hoped she was right, but he was not very confident. In his opinion the council was not likely to be so easily persuaded, but he did not want to dampen his mother's enthusiasm.

The man from the council came and was very polite, but he did not think the dust was a

43

health hazard. He couldn't explain it, but he thought perhaps it was the vibration from the heavy lorries and juggernauts which sometimes used the road. He said it was the landlord's job to see to any repairs which might be necessary. Finally, he said they did not qualify for a council house, and went away.

Colin's mother wouldn't go near Colin's bedroom, and she forbade Colin to go in there. She was very quiet that evening, and Colin had the nasty feeling that she was getting depressed again. They watched "Some Mothers Do 'Ave 'Em" and she didn't laugh once.

Suddenly she said "You're not going back in that room. Not ever! There's something sinister about that dust."

"Sinister?" His stomach lurched fearfully.

"Yes, sinister. I'm not cleaning it up again. I'm going to put a film in the camera and I'm going to take a photo of that room. I want a photo of that dust."

"A photo?" He was baffled.

"For the newspapers, silly! I shall send it to one of the papers and they'll send a reporter and—"

"But where shall I sleep in the meantime? If I can't use my room?"

"In the lounge on the sofa – and take that look off your face!"

He tried his best to make her change her mind, but she was determined.

She said, "If your father were alive he'd have done something to get us out of this place. Well, he's not here, but I am and I'm going to do something."

She fetched blankets from the airing cupboard and made up a bed on the sofa. It was surprisingly comfortable, but Colin found it hard to sleep. It was quiet at the back of the house and he missed the roar of the traffic as it thundered past his bedroom window.

He dozed off at last at about half past twelve. For an hour everything was still and silent.

At half past one there was a terrific crash and the whole house shook.

Colin awoke with his heart pounding, and screamed at once for his mother. He thought that a bomb had fallen; that a third world war had broken out.

"Mum!"

He rushed to the door and saw that his mother was also terrified. She was very pale, and her hands shook as they fastened the belt of her dressing gown.

"It came from your room," she told him and cautiously she opened the door.

What they saw made them gasp with shock. The cab of a large truck had wedged itself across

45

the room, crushing the bed where Colin would normally have been sleeping. The front wall of the room had been completely demolished, and the air was thick with a grey dust from the broken masonry. In the cab a middle-aged man was slumped in the driver's seat, with blood trickling from a cut over his right eye.

His mother screamed "He's dead! Oh Lord! What shall we do?"

Colin ran into the lounge and dialled 999 as neighbours began to gather in the street outside, appalled and shocked by the accident. His mother was still staring at the dust which was spreading into the hall and drifting into the lounge.

"The dust!" she whispered. "The grey dust! It was a warning, Colin. A warning from your father!"

Within minutes the police arrived, followed very shortly after by an ambulance and finally the fire brigade. It took nearly an hour to free the driver and then he was loaded into the back of the ambulance. He was conscious now, but suffering from the severe chest pains that had suddenly gripped him, making him swerve off the road.

"Heart attack, but he'll live!" the ambulance man assured Colin as he climbed into the driver's seat. "Don't you worry about him."

The police asked Colin and his mother for further details of what had happened, and then they were both taken into a neighbour's house and overwhelmed with kindness.

Colin was made comfortable on a camp bed in the boxroom, but as the dawn came up he was still wide awake. In spite of his narrow escape he was smiling up at the ceiling, happier than he had felt for a long time. He knew in his heart that everything would turn out well because his mother was now convinced that her dead husband had been watching over them. He had not deserted them after all. Colin muttered "Thanks, Dad!" He could see it all so clearly now. Because they were homeless the council would offer them a house with a rent they could afford. They would be safe and happy.

He closed his eyes and whispered again, "Thanks, Dad!".

And could almost hear his father answer, "That's OK, son!"

JUST CAUSE OR
IMPEDIMENT

Just Cause or Impediment

Suzanne had never liked him, although she did not know why. Perhaps he was too nice to her, which made her suspicious. Perhaps he was too perfect. He came from a wealthy family in South Africa. His sister was a brilliant doctor and his father had been a famous lawyer. Now both his parents were dead, although they had seen photographs of them. Of course, Pat was crazy about him, and if Suzanne said anything critical Pat simply thought she was jealous.

Alec Turner was too handsome, with bright blue eyes and a firm mouth and wonderful wavy blond hair. He could have been a male model. Pat often boasted about him. Not to Suzanne, though, because Suzanne always went rather quiet when Alec Turner was mentioned.

It was his eyes. There was something indefinable in his eyes that made Suzanne wary. She did not want Pat to marry him, but Pat was determined. When the wedding was announced the family were delighted – except for Suzanne.

"Do please be nice to him, Susie," Pat begged.

"He really likes you, you know, and he wants you to be a bridesmaid."

Suzanne tried to wriggle out of it, but it seemed she would be the only one. He had nieces and nephews in South Africa, but the family would not be attending the wedding.

"It's too far and too expensive," her mother explained when Suzanne said she thought it odd. "It's a long way and it wouldn't be fair if some of them came and others were left behind."

The preparations went ahead. Suzanne tried to sound enthusiastic, despite the niggling doubt at the back of her mind. Her dress was apricot silk, and she was to carry a posy of freesias. The dress suited her rather well so she *did* make an effort to look on the bright side. They were hiring a marquee which would be erected in the grounds of a nearby hotel. Mum had called in caterers to provide the food.

"I just can't be worrying about sandwiches and vol-au-vents," her mother explained, admiring herself in the mirror. Her outfit was in cornflower blue with a rather exotic hat in blue and white straw. Poor Dad would have to wear a "penguin" suit with tails. He hated the idea, but Pat was adamant.

Mum would do the flowers herself – she had been to Flower Arranging classes for years, and Dad insisted that this way they could get some of their money back! She chose chrysanthemums in apricot, bronze and white, and there would be plenty of trailing greenery and ferns. There was a vase on either side of the altar rail and she spent ages drawing diagrams about how the flowers would look. It drove Dad berserk and he told Suzanne not to get married until she was at least thirty!

At last the great day arrived. Suzanne woke with a nasty, fluttery feeling in her stomach. She did not want Pat to marry Alec Turner, but she was helpless to stop her. She'd have to grin and bear it and hope for the best.

Pat went off to the hairdressers and Mum and Dad went off to the hotel to make sure the marquee was where it should be. Suzanne brushed her hair and then put on her dress. She had to admit that she did look rather good. She just did not *feel* good.

She went to Pat's room to help her dress. This seemed to take a very long time, but when she had finished, Pat looked radiant in a froth of white. Suzanne suddenly realized that she would be leaving them, and home, and the family would be changed for ever. Not Mum, Dad, Pat and Suzanne but Mum, Dad and Suzanne. For a moment she hated Alec Turner. Then she reminded herself that Pat loved him. That was what was important.

Half an hour later, the church was filling up. The bride's friends and relations sat one side of the church and the groom's family sat the other side. Only that side was empty!

Suzanne, waiting nervously in the church porch, could not believe it.

"Hasn't he got any friends?" she demanded in a hoarse whisper, but Mum simply shrugged and hurried to her place. Alec Turner arrived with the best man, and Suzanne smiled dutifully and shook hands with them both.

Then Dad arrived with Pat, and the special music started as they walked down the aisle. Suzanne walked behind, taking care not to step on her sister's train.

"Do you take this woman to be your bride . . ."

Suzanne felt a shiver run through her, but tried to ignore it. This man would be her brother-in-law. He would be an uncle to her children when she had some. She *must* try to like him.

". . . To love and to cherish till death us do part . . ."

Suzanne glanced at her mother. She was looking wonderfully happy, and dabbing her eyes with a handkerchief. Her grandmother was also beaming fondly at Pat and Alec.

Suddenly Suzanne shivered again, and this time she realized that she was *cold*. Yet it was July, and outside the sun was blazing down. From the corner of her eye she saw her grandmother turn up the collar of her new linen suit. Glancing around her she saw that several people were hunching their shoulders or pulling their collars closer to their necks. Why on earth should it be so cold?

Ahead of her Pat shivered suddenly, and Alec crossed his arms over his chest. The temperature in the church was dropping rapidly. Even the vicar noticed it, breaking off in the middle of a sentence to stare round the church, a puzzled expression on his face.

Suzanne's fingers were really cold now, so cold that she was afraid she might drop the freesias. She saw Pat whisper something to Alec, and then the vicar spoke to them and they all looked around the church, mystified. Suzanne was watching the flowers on either side of the altar rail. *They were beginning to droop with the cold. The stems sagged and the petals began to curl up. Even the greenery seemed limp.*

"What's happening?" cried Mum in a loud whisper but the rest of the guests were too busy trying to keep warm, and nobody answered her.

Alec Turner was staring at the church window. Suzanne followed his gaze and she saw with a frisson of fear that they were frosting over!

Alec said, "Oh my God!"

The vicar said "This is most unusual. Absolutely

55

inexplicable!" And his voice shook. He made an effort to carry on as though nothing was happening, but finally he faltered to a stop.

Suzanne had the strangest feeling that someone *or something* was standing behind the vicar. A shadowy figure. The figure of a woman. Alec Turner saw it too and his hands went up to cover his face. He groaned loudly and sank to his knees. The apparition, if that is what it was, remained for a moment, faint and indistinct – and then it vanished. Incredibly, no one else seemed to have seen it. Certainly Pat had paid it no attention. She was staring in dismay at her bouquet, which had withered in her hands. With a cry of fear she suddenly threw it to the floor.

There were anxious murmurs from the guests, and Pat turned to look at them. She was very pale and Suzanne's heart ached for her. Now there was ice forming on the windows and a deep hoar frost covered the floor and crept up over pews and along the altar rail. The newly polished brass candlesticks dimmed over and the sunlight disappeared. The interior of the church grew dark and gloomy and one or two people hurried out.

Pat turned to Alec, tears in her eyes. "What is it? I don't understand."

He shrugged, not trusting himself to speak. He looked guilty and ill at ease.

"I can't go through with it!" he cried out, and turned and ran down the aisle and out of the church.

There was a stunned silence and then Pat slumped to the ground. Suzanne, Mum and Gran rushed forward to help her. Dad, after a moment's hesitation, hurried after the fleeing bridegroom.

The day was ruined, naturally. The wedding was cancelled and all the guests went home. All the wedding presents would have to be returned. Pat did not shed a single tear, but she changed overnight from a happy young woman to a sad shadow of the sister Suzanne had known and loved all her life.

Time passed and the family did their best to help Pat to put the past behind her. Suzanne began to think that she would never recover from Alec Turner's cruel betrayal. Pat became so depressed that she was unable to work, and instead moped at home all day reading in her room. When she did join the family she was morose and irritable. She tortured herself with unanswerable questions. "Why did he leave me? What happened that day?"

For a long time there were no answers, but one day, out of the blue, the truth finally emerged. Suzanne was watching the news half-heartedly while trying to do her homework when a familiar name jolted her into attention.

" . . . *Alec Turner, a man in his thirties, has confessed to the murder of his wife, Elaine Mary Turner, at his home three years ago. Early this morning he led police to her body which was buried in woodlands close to his home in Berkshire. The man claims that the ghost of his wife has haunted him ever since her death. Detective Inspector Lawrence said this afternoon that the man was in a highly emotional state and will be receiving medical treatment prior to his trial . . .*"

She stared at the photograph. There was no mistake. It was the same man. "A murderer!" she whispered, hardly able to believe it. "Alec Turner is a *murderer!*"

She jumped up from the table and rushed to the foot of the stairs. "Pat! Come quickly! Alec Turner's on the television!"

It seemed unbelievable, but the news was repeated in the newspaper headlines the following morning. There was a photograph of Alec Turner (whose real name was John Reddy) and details of the crime. He had strangled his wife after a quarrel, and had taken her body to the woods in the boot of his car.

Pat read and re-read the article and then laid down the paper. Her face was very white but her relief was obvious.

"That could have been me," she said, and burst into tears. She cried for a long time, but they were healing tears and long overdue. In a matter of weeks she was herself again and able to pick up the threads of her life.

At the trial several months later there were more surprises. "Alec Turner" had never been in South Africa. His father had never been a lawyer and never would be. His sister, the brilliant doctor, was a married woman who lived in Orpington and worked part-time in a greengrocer's shop.

Nobody could explain the events at the church that had led to Alec Turner's disappearance on the day of the wedding but Suzanne had her own views on the subject. She *knew* it was Elaine's ghost she had seen in the church.

Suzanne also understood at last what she had seen in Alec's eyes that had troubled her.

It was murder.

The
Children

The Children

When Diana's mother was suddenly taken ill with appendicitis, they rushed her to hospital. Diana's father was at work all day, so Diana was sent down to Winchelsea to stay with her grandmother who had moved into a new cottage by the sea. At least, it was new to her, but it was actually quite old. It had creepers over the wall and the gate was falling off its hinges.

"There are some tiles missing from the roof, too," Gran told her. "I shall have to get a man along to fix them before the winter."

But she was very proud of her new home, and took Diana on a tour of the cottage.

"This is the lounge – or as they would have called it – the parlour. The kitchen is through here." She led the way. "See the lovely old Aga. I've always wanted one. They keep the kitchen so cosy in the bad weather."

Diana nodded dutifully. She was too polite to say that she preferred her grandmother's previous house. She admired the big dresser with its blue and white china and the floor which was paved in slabs of stone.

"I know it's old-fashioned," said Gran, "but that's what I liked about it. I shan't change a thing. They wouldn't want me to."

Diana followed her up the steep staircase and into a very ancient bathroom. The iron bath was a funny shape and stood on four little legs shaped like lions' claws.

Her grandmother said proudly, "You couldn't buy a bath like that now for love or money!"

Diana murmured something and wondered who would want to buy such a terrible bath.

The two bedrooms had sloping roofs and they looked out on to a large field. Beyond the field was the sea.

One of the bedrooms was Gran's. The spare one was for visitors.

"I wasn't expecting visitors quite so soon," Gran admitted. "The room's not really ready yet. Not much furniture and no carpet, but I expect you can manage."

The room certainly was rather sparsely furnished. It had a small camp bed made up with a thin mattress and a plump pillow, all covered by an old patchwork quilt.

Diana said, "Have I seen that quilt before?"

"No. I found it here when I moved in. They didn't want me to throw it out so I gave it a good wash. It came up a treat."

Diana looked at it doubtfully. Some of the seams were coming undone and the colours were very faded.

There was a small chest of drawers against one wall and a chair in the corner. A mirror hung on the wall beside a framed sampler.

Seeing her looking at this with interest, Gran explained eagerly. "Victorian and Edwardian children used to stitch samplers when they learned needlework. They stitched words into the design. Usually their own names and date of birth. That was done by Dorky."

"Door key?" Diana stared. "Was that her name?"

Her grandmother laughed. "Not door key. Dorky. Short for Dorcas. She was only eight years old when she started it. She told me—"

She stopped abruptly, and Diana missed the expression in her grandmother's eyes. She had discovered a rag doll stuffed into the bottom drawer of the chest. The doll had hair made of string and her cloth face had a nose, mouth and eyes sewn on with coloured wools. The long dress was edged with torn lace and the petticoats hid pantaloons.

"Was this Dorky's, do you think?" Diana asked curiously.

"No, no. That belonged to Sarah. Her cousin.

At least, it was given to them to share but of course they quarrelled over it. Children can't share things like dolls. It was finally given to Sarah and Dorky was given another doll, but—"

"How on earth do you know all this?" Diana asked.

Her grandmother hesitated then spoke carefully. "Look, Diana. You mustn't worry about things that happen here. It's nothing bad. Just a bit of fun. They don't mean any harm."

Diana looked at her grandmother suspiciously. "What do you mean? What things? Who don't mean any harm?"

Gran laughed nervously. "Oh, it's nothing. Forget I said anything. Probably nothing will happen. But if it does—" She stopped again, obviously troubled.

"Gran!" Diana was by now thoroughly alarmed. "Is something awful going to happen?"

"Of course not!" Gran smiled. "Would I agree to let you stay here if I thought you'd be in any danger? Forget all about it. I'm just a silly old woman. Now you unpack and I'll go down and get some tea. I've bought a swiss roll. I know that's your favourite."

She left Diana feeling puzzled and rather nervous. Her grandmother was not old, she was fifty-eight, and she was certainly not silly. There was something bothering her.

"I suppose she'll tell me in her own good time," Diana said to herself, and she began to unpack. Her clothes went into the various drawers of the chest. She put underwear on the top shelf; shorts and tee shirts in the next one down; jumpers, socks, odds and ends in the next. The bottom drawer was empty except for the old doll. Her wellington boots went in the corner. There was no table, so her hairbrush and comb went on the chair. When she had finished she crossed the room to take another look at the sampler.

DORCAS MARY LEIGH Born 1st October 1885

There was a border of cross stitch and a few daisy-like flowers. Looking at it, she tried to imagine the little girl, only eight years old, her head bent over her sewing. It gave her a feeling of sadness to think that now she was gone for ever. The young Dorky must have grown into an old lady and then died.

"Long before I was born!" said Diana.

She went downstairs and shared a delicious tea with her grandmother. Then they went for a long walk, over the field to the beach. Here the wind was whipping the waves and they were soon caught by a gust of spray which sent them hurrying back from the sea's edge.

On the way home Gran said suddenly, "I have strange dreams here. I dream there are children playing in the field. They dance in a ring and they sing. You might dream it, too. I'm just warning you."

Diana laughed and said "Do people share the same dreams? I've never heard of that."

"Oh yes they do!" said her grandmother. "So if you dream it, don't let it worry you."

"No, I won't."

She went to bed that night not knowing what to expect, but nothing happened. She woke in the morning from what seemed to be a dreamless sleep. So her grandmother's strange warning had been quite unnecessary.

With a sense of relief she jumped out of bed and ran to the window. The field outside was empty. The sky was blue. It was going to be a good day. She went to the chair to collect her brush and comb and stopped in surprise. The chair was empty. "Funny!" she muttered.

A glance round the room did not reveal the brush and comb. On an impulse she went to the chest and pulled open one drawer after another. The brush and comb were in the bottom drawer with the doll.

"I must be going mad!" grinned Diana. "I don't remember putting them there."

She washed, cleaned her teeth and brushed her hair. Gran was already in the kitchen, where the kettle whistled gently on the hob of the Aga.

They spent the day shopping and gardening, and in the evening they watched the television. Diana had forgotten about the brush and comb incident and went yawning up to bed. She was surprised to see Sarah's doll lying on top of the bed.

"Gran!" she smiled. Obviously her grandmother had put it there. But why? Did she hope Diana would take a fancy to it? She ran downstairs and put her head round the door. "Is she for me?" she asked.

Gran looked up. "Is who for you?"

"The doll. You put her on the bed and I thought—"

"I did?"

"Didn't you?"

"Oh! Oh yes. Of course."

"Did you mean me to have her?"

Gran looked shocked. "To keep? Oh no, dear! I couldn't possibly. She would never forgive me."

"Who wouldn't?"

"Oh dear!" The familiar face wrinkled in dismay. "I didn't want to say anything. You see, Sarah comes to me. They all do. They tell me things. Sarah would never part with the doll.

69

I expect she's lent it to you. Just while you're staying here."

Diana regarded her grandmother steadily, trying not to show her anxiety. It had finally dawned on her that her grandmother's mind was disturbed.

"They come to you?" she repeated as calmly as she could.

"That's right. They're so sweet. So innocent. I haven't the heart to send them away. They play and they tease me a little. Hide things from me. Things like that." Her expression was worried. "They are totally without malice."

"They're ghosts, you mean?"

"I suppose they *are* ghosts, but I sometimes wonder if they know they're ghosts. I never mention it. I wouldn't want to upset them. Poor little mites. They died young, you see."

Diana's heart sank. She was going to have to tell her parents about poor Gran. She might even have to go into a home or a hospital. Presumably there was some treatment for delusions? She said carefully, "How many children are there? And how did they die?"

Her grandmother sat down and began to count them off on her fingers.

"There's Sarah, of course, and Dorky. They died in this house. There was a storm and a tree blew down on their bedroom. That's your room."

Diana shuddered, but her grandmother went

on quite cheerfully. "Annie is another cousin. She died of consumption when she was only eleven. Billy's the baby. Only four when he fell down the stairs." She tutted with exasperation. "Children had such short lives in those days. It's a wonder any of them survived. You might hear him laughing. I usually hear him on the stairs. A real gurgle!" She smiled at the memory. "He's the only boy, so they spoil him a bit. Then there's Jennet. She was earlier. She lived in the cottage in the seventeenth century. She was nearly fifteen when she died. Ate some rotten mutton and it poisoned her."

Diana sat poker-faced as she listened to the incredible catalogue. Poor Gran! She had had some kind of mental breakdown. She was quite mad.

Her grandmother smiled. "So now you know why I shall never be lonely."

Diana's throat was suddenly dry, and she could only nod and smile. She decided that she would write to her mother, but later changed her mind. Her mother was in hospital and had enough worries of her own. Instead she would telephone her father at the first opportunity. She must explain what had happened to his mother. He would know what to do. In the meantime she must keep her grandmother as calm as she could.

That night she lay in bed wide awake, wondering how to break the bad news to her father. He and his mother were very fond of each other and he would be horrified to hear of her breakdown. He wouldn't want her to go into a home, but there was no room for anyone else in their small flat. Could they afford a bigger house? she wondered. Or might they be able to pay for a trained nurse to live with Gran in the cottage?

Suddenly her ears caught an unfamiliar sound and she sat up in bed. It sounded like singing, but that was impossible. She looked at her watch and saw that it was just after midnight. No one would be singing at this hour.

But the sound grew louder and clearer. Diana got out of bed – and had another shock. The doll was now sitting on the floor in the corner of the room where the wellingtons had been. The wellingtons had gone!

Diana swallowed hard and tried to convince herself that she was not afraid. She must have moved them herself and then forgotten about it. But her grandmother's words returned to mock her.

"They play and tease me a little . . . They hide things . . ."

Aloud Diana said "It's impossible!" And almost ran to the window. She had hoped to see an empty field. Instead she saw a wavering ring of dancing children of assorted ages. They were singing a song she didn't recognise, but she could pick out each child. Jennet, the oldest, with long brown hair; Annie, a little shorter; Billy was, as Grandmother had said, only a baby. The two younger girls would be Dorky and Sarah.

"No!" she shouted at the top of her voice. She must be imagining it and yet even at this distance she could see that their clothes were old fashioned and that their feet were bare. She flung open the window and shouted again.

"No! No! Go away!"

Her words reached them and they faltered in their dance. The circle broke up and five startled faces were turned towards her.

For several seconds they stared up at her appealingly, then they linked hands again and began to dance. This time they were silent but their dance grew faster. Still reluctant to admit what she saw, Diana blinked her eyes and suddenly they were nothing more than a swirling ring of colour against the moonlit grass. A swirling mist that grew fainter and then vanished. There was a knock at the door and Grandma stood in the doorway in her dressing gown.

Diana cried, "I saw them, Gran! All of them! I did!"

The words tumbled out incoherently as she tried to describe what she had seen.

"Was it real, Gran? Did I see them?"

There was despair in her voice because if she had imagined it all then she was also mad.

Her grandmother put an arm round her and held her tight.

"You did see them," she said gently. "They often come back. We shouldn't begrudge them their few moments of pleasure."

Diana gasped. "How can you be so calm about it? You see ghosts and you aren't afraid? Oh Gran, I was terrified. My heart's still pounding!"

Gran said "But remember I have seen them many times. I've had time to get used to the idea. You will, too, in time."

She made a cup of Ovaltine and they sat in the kitchen sipping it slowly. Their hands were round the mugs, grateful for a little warmth and reassurance.

Gran said, "They had such short lives, poor little things. I rather like the idea that they still live here; that they don't consider me an intruder."

Diana looked up into the kindly, familiar face. "They're lucky to have you. And so am I!"

As they finally went up the stairs to bed they heard an unmistakable chuckle.

"That's Billy!" whispered Gran, and she and Diana smiled like two conspirators.

The next day Diana wrote a brief letter to her father. She told him that she had settled in well, that the cottage was very nice and that Gran sent her love. They hoped Mum would soon be well. There was no mention of her grandmother's children. That was a secret between them and would remain so for ever.

THE EMPTY
HOUSE

The Empty House

The house next door had been empty for a long time; longer than Steven could remember and he was nearly ten years old. When Fiona, his cousin, came to stay, she demanded to know all about it.

"I don't know," he told her. "I only know I'm not allowed to go in there. Not even in the garden."

"Why not?"

"I told you – I don't know why. It's just not allowed."

Fiona looked at him scornfully. She was two years older than Steven and inclined to be bossy. She went to find Steven's mother.

"Why can't we explore next door?" she asked.

Steven's mother hesitated. "It's not safe," she said at last. "The people who lived there were not very nice and the place has got a bad reputation. That's why it's been empty for so long."

Fiona scowled. "But can't we just go and look through the windows?"

"No you can't!"

Fiona reported back to Steven, who said, "I told you so!"

But Fiona was not the sort of person to give in too easily. "I know what we'll do," she said. "We'll ask the man who lives on the other side of the house. Come on!"

And she rushed out and hurried along the street with Steven trailing reluctantly behind her. Her luck was in. Mr Berry, a retired fireman, was tying up some roses in his front garden. Fiona introduced herself and then, quite casually, mentioned the empty house.

At once Mr Berry frowned. "You'd best keep away from there," he warned. "There's something evil about that place. Something rotten."

Steven's heart began to race, but Fiona wanted to know more.

The old man pursed his lips. "Well, all I can say is that you wouldn't get me in there. Not for love or money! I went down those basement steps once, looking for my cat. Henry, I call him. Big fierce tabby, he is. Tough as old boots. I went down the steps and I heard—" He shook his head. "I heard digging."

"*Digging*?" Both children spoke at the same time.

"Aye. Digging. I distinctly heard the sound of a spade hitting the ground, over and over. Bearing in mind, of course, that the house had been empty for some years then."

"Oh dear!" said Steven nervously.

Mr Berry lowered his voice. "And then, of course, I remembered the story. Folks say that an old man died there – poisoned by his grown-up nephew."

Suddenly Steven didn't want to hear any more. He knew he'd have nightmares. But Fiona said, "Go on, Mr Berry!"

"Well, they say this old man disappeared and his body was never found. The nephew said he'd wandered away; that his mind was gone. But the folks who lived in my house before I did, they said they heard a lot of digging in the basement and they reckoned the old man was buried there. It's the nephew that haunts the place. Guilt, you see. The old man's money did him no good. He went mad." He pointed meaningfully to his forehead. "A few years later he threw himself into the river and drowned."

Steven shuddered. "What a dreadful story!" he whispered, genuinely shocked by the tragedy.

Fiona's eyes had almost popped out of her head. "And is it still there? The old man's body?" she asked.

Mr Berry shrugged. "I don't know and I don't want to know," he told them. "They're dead and gone and let that be the end of them. My advice to you two is to stay away from that house."

To Steven's relief Fiona said, "Oh we will, Mr Berry." But she winked at Steven behind the old man's back and Steven's heart sank. He knew that Fiona would never be satisfied until she had explored the empty house.

That night, just as he was settling himself for sleep, there was a tap on his bedroom door. Fiona came in wearing her coat over her pyjamas. She looked very odd, but Steven was in no mood for laughing.

"Come on!" she said. "We're going next door."

Steven began to protest that he thought they should take Mr Berry's advice and stay away. Fiona tossed her head.

"You really are a baby!" she told him. "Nearly ten years old and afraid of a few ghosts! I had no idea you were such a scaredy-cat."

"But we'll get into terrible trouble if they find out."

"They won't find out – unless you're stupid enough to tell them. Oh, do get a move on! And don't make a noise."

Steven wondered if he dared make a noise deliberately so that his parents would be alerted. No, he decided reluctantly. Fiona would never forgive him.

After a little more argument, Steven gave in. He decided that since he would have to go he would get it over as quickly as possible. He slid from his bed and pulled on his jeans and a sweater and pushed his feet into his trainers.

Fiona had a torch and she also carried a heavy spanner.

"What's that for?" Steven asked.

"You never know," she answered mysteriously. "I found it in the garage." And she thrust it into his hand.

Steven's bedroom was on the ground floor, so it was a simple matter to open the window and jump down into the moonlit garden. Silently they made their way over the grass and climbed the low fence that separated the two houses. At the side of the empty house, worn steps led down to a basement.

Steven had an idea. He pushed ahead of Fiona and rattled the door handle.

"Oh dear! It's locked," he said, trying to sound disappointed.

Fiona was not deterred. "Of course it is," she said. "That's what the spanner's for, you twit!"

Before Steven could protest she had snatched it from him. With one quick blow she had dislodged the rusty lock. Then she handed the spanner back to him.

Even now Steven did his best to dissuade her from entering the house, but she laughed at his objections and called him a coward. Pushing open the door, she stepped inside. Steven drew a deep breath and prepared to follow her, but before he could do so the door slammed in his face.

At the same moment Fiona screamed.

It was a bloodcurdling sound that sent shivers up his spine.

"I'm coming!" he shouted and began to push at the door. He beat on it with his fist and threw his weight against it but with no result. It seemed to be locked on the inside. But who could have locked it? Surely not Fiona.

"Fiona! Open the door!"

He waited, but there was no reply. Instead he caught a sound that made his blood freeze. He heard the sound of a spade striking the ground.

"Fiona! What are you doing? It's me, Steven. Open the door!"

A man's voice cried out "Dig! Dig! Faster. Dig, you little fool!"

And quite distinctly he heard Fiona sobbing.

Almost paralysed with fright, Steven wondered what to do. If he went back for his parents they would blame her for the episode and she would get into serious trouble.

"But she's in serious trouble already!" he told himself desperately. There was a window alongside the door but it was covered with dirt and he could see nothing inside the basement.

"Dig, damn you!" the man's voice continued

and Fiona's terrified sobbing galvanized Steven into action.

He swung the spanner and smashed the grimy window.

At once there was silence. A silence that was almost as terrifying as the noise that had preceded it. The silence lengthened until Steven ended it.

"Fiona!" he whispered.

He peered in through the window, avoiding the jagged glass, but at that moment the door opened and Fiona staggered out. She was shaking all over and could hardly speak. Seeing him, she gasped with relief and threw herself into his astonished arms.

"Home," she stammered and somehow he helped her back across the fence and into the safety of his bedroom.

She was a pitiful sight. Her hair was dishevelled and full of cobwebs, her face was blotched and tearstained, and there was an angry-looking blister on her right hand.

"What happened?" he asked gently but she shook her head, refusing to speak.

Quietly he padded along the passage to the bathroom and returned with a wet flannel and some soap. Gently he washed her face and hands. He put soothing cream on her blistered hand. He found a comb and tidied her hair, but nothing could erase the terror from her eyes.

It was nearly an hour before she recovered enough to go back to her own room. In all that time she did not speak a word.

Next morning, she made a tremendous effort to behave normally, but Steven's mother was concerned.

"You look terrible, Fiona," she told her. "Aren't you well?"

Fiona avoided her eyes.

"I've got a headache" she said. "I didn't sleep well. I – I had a nightmare."

"Poor you," said Steven's mother. "Well, take it easy today. No rushing about."

Steven said, "I'll keep an eye on her," and smiled at his cousin. To his surprise she smiled back. Not her usual superior smile but a grateful smile; the smile of one friend to another.

Fiona never would speak of that terrible night and Steven never did know what had happened in the empty house. In one way he was sorry, but in another he was glad. Some things are too awful to put into words, and he was old enough to understand that Fiona's ordeal was one of them. Neither of them ever went near the empty house again. As Mr Berry had said, it was an evil place and they had learned to their cost that evil is best left undisturbed.

NUMBER
SEVENTY-TWO

Number Seventy-Two

"I can hardly believe it!" cried Sandra's grandmother. "It looks exactly the same – except that the trees are bigger!"

Sandra was not impressed with the street. The houses were tall and terraced, and the brickwork was grimy. Crumbling steps led up to each front door, and in the lowest one of these steps there was a rusting iron grid.

"That lets air into the cellars," Grandma said, in answer to Sandra's question. She was staring up at the top windows of number seventy-two, shading her eyes from the sunlight.

The man beside her said, "Well, shall we go in?" and led the way up the steps.

Sandra didn't like him. He was an estate agent who was showing them over the property because Grandma had pretended she wanted to buy it. Sandra's grandmother had been born in the house and the family had still been there when the Second World War started. As soon as she had spotted the house in the estate agent's window, she had decided she must see it again and had insisted that Sandra come too.

Grandma was now looking at the front garden with a disapproving expression on her face. There were weeds everywhere and the paving slabs which made up the front path were cracked and uneven.

"There used to be roses," she told the estate agent. "They used to be the best in the whole street." To Sandra she said, "Your great-grand-father had a way with roses."

The estate agent was fiddling with a bunch of keys, trying to find the one that fitted the lock on the peeling front door.

"The knocker's gone, too," said Grandma. "Always polished, that knocker was. A lion's head, all in brass. I used to love it. I could just reach it if I stood on tiptoe."

They went into the large, airless hall which was tiled in black and white squares.

Grandma was smiling to herself.

"I used to push my dolls up and down this hall in their pram," she said with a sigh. "It only seems like yesterday and yet, here I am, fifty-six years old and not getting any younger."

Really, thought Sandra. Grandma could be very silly at times. She stole a look at the estate agent's face and thought he looked rather bored.

"I'll start at the top," Grandma told him, "and work my way down."

Sandra decided to let them get on with it.

"I'll stay down here," she said firmly. "I'll explore on my own."

Her grandmother nodded vaguely, too wrapped up in her memories to object.

The estate agent gave Sandra a sour look and said, "Well, don't do any damage, young lady," and followed Grandma up the creaking stairs.

Sandra was glad to see them go. If her grandmother was going to ramble on about her childhood Sandra didn't want to hear it. The past was boring, in her opinion. Who cared what had happened all those years ago? Grandma had told a whopping lie to the estate agent, saying that she wanted to buy the house so that the entire family could live under one roof. Sandra knew that she didn't have any money – at least, not enough to buy a house in London – but Grandma had waved aside her protests. And here they were.

As the footsteps overhead grew fainter, Sandra took a quick look in the rooms on either side of the wide hall. One was obviously a bedroom, for there was a faded patch on the wallpaper in the shape of a bedhead.

The other rooms were equally shabby, with a musty smell that might have been mildew.

There was a kitchen at the back which looked

out on to a large but overgrown garden. Sandra tried and failed to imagine her grandmother playing there as a child.

In the corner of the kitchen there were two doors. One went into a cupboard full of mice droppings and cobwebs. The other led down to the cellar by way of very rickety wooden steps.

Sandra hesitated. If she went upstairs to ask permission, someone would forbid her to go down those stairs. She decided she would go anyway.

Clinging on to the ancient rope handrail, she began to make her way down the steps. There was no light switch and it looked rather gloomy, but Sandra told herself that she could always turn back if she changed her mind.

Below her, in the darkness, there was a scampering sound, but she wasn't afraid of mice so went slowly on, one step at a time.

Suddenly one of the steps collapsed under her weight and with a cry of fright she slithered feet first towards the cellar. She seemed to be falling for such a long time! There was a rush of air past her, blowing her long fair hair across her face, so that she couldn't see.

All at once she landed on something soft and lay for a moment, winded by the fall. At first everything was dark, but then a small torch was switched on and Sandra saw to her astonishment that she was not alone. There was a young boy sitting on a camp bed opposite her!

"What's up, Rose?" he asked. He was shielding the torchlight with his hand and he glanced over his shoulder towards the iron grille set high up in the wall. She glanced round the cellar and could dimly make out the grid which she had seen from the outside of the house.

"I'm not sure—" Sandra began, but at that moment there was an urgent tapping at the grid and a man's face appeared.

"Put that light out!" he said crossly. "How many times do I have to tell you? Want to get us all killed, do you?"

Sandra stared at him open-mouthed, but the boy switched off the light and said "Sorry, Mr Burke."

"I should think so!" This time the voice was less stern and he added "OK, are you?"

Sandra said, "I fell down the steps," but nobody paid her any attention.

The man said, "No sign of anything yet. Perhaps we'll be lucky tonight. Perhaps they'll drop their bombs somewhere else. But then again, pigs might fly!"

Chuckling to himself, he was suddenly gone, and to Sandra's surprise she realized that there was no daylight coming in through the grid.

She had fallen on to a camp bed, and now she

felt herself for broken bones but found none. Somehow she had survived that long fall. It was all very puzzling and rather frightening.

"What was that man wearing on his head?" she asked.

The boy said, "His helmet, of course! Don't be such a goose, Rose! And his name's Mr Burke."

"But who is he?"

There was a moment's silence and then the boy said, "You know as well as I do. He's the Air Raid Warden, so don't start being silly. You know what Mum said about trying to scare me."

"I'm not trying to scare you," Sandra told him. "And my name's not Rose."

"Then I'm not Gerry. I'm – I'm Popeye!"

Before Sandra could work this out there was a loud wailing noise and at once the boy cried "Where's Sammy?"

"Sammy who?"

"Oh Rose! You are a beast! I shall tell!"

She heard him groping around on the floor as outside a loud droning noise grew louder and more threatening.

He called desperately. "Sammy? Where are you? Oh Sam!" Then added. "He must be upstairs! Oh Rose, he might be in the garden! He'll get killed!"

"But who is he?" she cried.

To her astonishment she felt a quick cuff on

the side of her head as the boy ran past her and began to climb the steps. He was making the noises people make to call cats, and she suddenly guessed that Sam was a pet cat. But how on earth could he be killed in the garden?

At that moment a door opened at the top of the steps and a woman rushed down, shooing the boy before her.

"Gerry! Rose! Stay very quiet and still, both of you!" she told them and the terror was evident in her trembling voice. "I don't want to frighten you but there's a German paratrooper in the garden. I just saw him land! Oh heavens! It gave me such a fright! I wish your father was here."

She pulled Sandra and the boy into her arms and began to cry, but the boy muttered, "I must get Sammy!" and broke free from her encircling arms. Before they realized what was happening, he was scrambling up the steps towards the door that led into the kitchen. Outside in the darkness heavy guns opened up, and somehow Sandra knew that they were trained on the enemy bombers caught in the glare of the searchlights. The noise was deafening, and she covered her ears as the first string of bombs fell on the city. The walls of the house shook as they exploded nearby, but regardless of the danger the woman was scrambling up the steps after the boy, shouting to him to come back. Sandra saw them both quite clearly in the light from the searchlights which filtered through the grid, filling the cellar with a ghostly light.

German paratroopers and bombs and guns? Sandra was totally confused. How could all this be happening with Grandma and the estate agent upstairs? Was she dreaming?

"Wait for me!" she cried and jumped from the bed. Whatever was happening, she didn't like it. She was frightened and she had no intention of being left alone in the cellar.

But now she found herself unable to walk; unable to take one step. Her legs refused to obey her and she felt as though she were choking. Then the light from the grid abruptly faded, leaving her in total darkness. The noise of the battle was fading too, but Sandra was too terrified to register the fact. She stood in the middle of the cellar and screamed for help.

"Sandra!"

The door had opened at the top of the steps and her grandmother and the estate agent were staring at her in surprise.

Sandra gulped for air, one hand to her rapidly beating heart.

Grandma said, "Was that you screaming?"

Sandra nodded, swamped with relief but lost for words.

The estate agent said sharply, "What's happened

to these steps? They were quite sound last time I showed someone round."

Sandra stammered out a few shaky sentences, explaining that she had fallen when the steps gave way.

Carefully she climbed back up while her grandmother told the estate agent that the house was in a dreadful state and she would not be considering buying it after all.

"It would cost the earth to put it right," she told him, and left him glowering on the pavement outside number seventy-two.

As they walked back to Grandma's flat a few streets away, Sandra recounted her adventure and her grandmother listened in stunned silence.

When Sandra had finished she gave a deep sigh and began to answer Sandra's unasked questions.

"Gerry was my brother," she began, "I hardly remember him, of course. I was only a child when he died. And as for Rose – well, I'm Rose."

"You?"

Her grandmother smiled. "I do have a name!" she told Sandra. "I wasn't christened 'Grandma'!"

But Sandra wasn't in the mood for humour. She was thinking rapidly.

"And the woman?" she asked. "Was that your mother?"

"Yes. Your great-grandmother, God bless her. She died before you were born. And poor Gerry died that very night. He was struck by a piece of shrapnel."

"Shrapnel?" Sandra repeated.

"Fragments of a shell or bomb," Grandma explained. "Apparently poor Gerry so loved that cat. He ran into the garden in the middle of an air raid to look for it. And while he was in the garden getting himself killed Sammy the cat was asleep in the armchair, as right as rain!"

Sandra frowned. "But how could I possibly see your brother and your mother if they've been dead for so long? Were they—" She swallowed nervously. "Were they ghosts?"

Grandma shook her head emphatically. "There's no such thing," she told Sandra. "You must have dreamed it all. I must have told you about it sometime and—"

"You never did," Sandra insisted. "I didn't even know you *had* a brother. And what about the German paratrooper? Did he find you in the cellar?"

To her surprise Grandma laughed. "Oh, that was so funny! Poor Ma never lived that down. You see, it wasn't a paratrooper at all. It was a barrage balloon that had been shot down. You know, one of those huge balloons that floated over London. The idea was that they would prevent enemy planes from coming too low. The balloons were made of a shiny material and as this one fell into the garden Ma thought it was a parachute!"

Sandra said, "I saw their ghosts! I'm sure I did. Or did I go back in time? It was all so real."

Grandma led the way up the stairs and fumbled in her bag for the key to her flat.

"You imagined it," she told Sandra. "You always did have a vivid imagination. Now, let's put the kettle on. I'm gasping for a 'cuppa'!"

Sandra followed her into the cosy kitchen and sank down on to a chair. She knew she had not imagined that scene in the cellar, but she couldn't explain it either. She only knew that she was terribly glad that they were *not* going to live in number seventy-two!

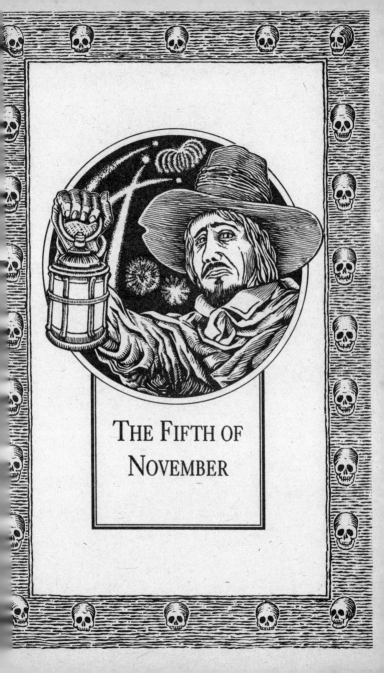

THE FIFTH OF
NOVEMBER

The Fifth of November

Listen well, my friend, for on a sudden I have decided. I crave revenge. For years I have watched their foolish antics while I choked with anger at their mockery. Bonfires! Pah! A few bits of wood and a paltry blaze and they stand open-mouthed at the spectacle. And all the children, wide eyed, gawping like little fish. They stare as though at a great and wondrous sight, and clap their little hands and shout with excitement so that I long to shake them until their teeth rattle.

You ask what I have decided. 'Tis this. To show them, once and for all, how it should have been. One almighty blast that should have brought down the Houses of Parliament and toppled the king from his throne. An explosion to rock and shock the world and change the course of history for ever. Not a few pathetic fireworks, popping and jumping and making pretty patterns in the air. Have you seen their rockets and Roman candles and suchlike? Mere trifles, I assure you. I spit on them. And as for the timid sparklers! Fit for a fairy wand and nothing more.

You see, my friend, *my* explosion will be the real thing. I see you smile. You think I can't do it; that I have no power because I am dead. Is that it? You are very wrong. Year by year, over the centuries, I have been saving what little power I have. Storing my phantom energies, you might say. Planning and waiting for the moment when I will recreate the event that should have taken place on that fateful day. The fifth of November. The glorious fifth . . .

I was robbed, you see, of my hour of glory. A so-called friend betrayed us, and even now I cannot be certain which of them played Judas. Thomas, maybe, or Robert – or Chris Wright with that devilish sense of humour. Although 'twas no joke, for it took us to our graves. God's wounds! I was so close to success. So very close. Had you been with me, my friend, you would have sworn the deed as good as done! The gunpowder was in place in the cellar for I had carried it there myself, barrel by beautiful barrel. What a sight for sore eyes! I covered the barrels well with sacking and heaped coal over them to hide them from sight. And, to make doubly sure, we piled bundles of firewood against them. They would never have been found except for . . . . But I digress.

Where shall I contrive my explosion, you ask. Ah! I have planned it well. I shall make my presence known at the little town of Rye in Sussex, a most pretty part of England. Pretty, but filled with fools who parade the streets on Guy Fawkes Day, carrying flaming torches, hiding their faces behind coloured masks. They dance and sing and rattle boxes in the faces of the onlookers. "Penny for the guy!" they cry, and the people toss coins and laugh as though my death was of no account. What do they care for my agony? Weeks in prison with no glimpse of God's sun – and then a hanging.

How will it be done? You *are* impatient. Listen well, my friends, for this is how. I shall walk in the procession as I walk every year, unrecognised in my tall hat and flowing cloak, with my pockets stuffed with gunpowder. There will be gunpowder in my knee-length boots and a certain quantity within my hat. My fingers inside the long gauntlet gloves will itch with the stuff and I shall feel it soft against my body. You grow pale, my friend, and with good reason. Yes. I shall be a walking powder keg and none will know. There will be no one to betray me this time. And the fools will jostle round me, laughing, but their hours will be numbered.

When we reach the flat green field beside the river – the one they call The Salts – I shall walk into the bonfire. Last year it was nigh on thirty feet high! A monstrous pile of dry tinder. Perfect for my purposes. The crowd will gather round, waiting for the moment when the fire begins. They will stand with their heads craned back, staring up at the figure perched on top. The mannikin they call Guy Fawkes! A sad creature of wood and straw, dressed to resemble me. To resemble *me*! Oh, they will pay for their insensitivity. They will pay dearly . . .

This, then, is the hour, my friend. The hour of my revenge. Watch closely, for we are nearly there! My heart still beats within me the way it did then. A hundred yards or so and I shall reach The Salts. Ah! There it is! And the fire burns well. A sight to warm my cold heart. Hear the crowd roar! But now they edge back, cowed by the rising heat so that an empty circle surrounds the fire. I step forward and my cloak swirls round me as they start to murmur among themselves. They begin to cry a warning, for I am too close to the flames and they are fearful for my safety. "Come back!" they shout. "You'll kill yourself!" What irony! I am already dead. I can come to no harm but they are in deadly peril. Poor timorous wretches. They know nothing of danger and death but they will learn. I shall blow them all to kingdom come and be waiting there to greet them with a smile.

Now I plunge into the flames and their cries are suddenly hushed, their eyes wide with disbelief. Only the crackle of the flames disturbs the terrible silence. Listen . . . . Listen . . . . Wait for the explosion . . .

WHOOSH!

A terrible, wondrous sound. God's teeth! 'Tis music to my ears. This is what I wanted. Oh! See them fall! Hear them scream! Would that it was the King's men running in such panic. That would have been a pretty sight. A sight to gladden the heart! Now they run as the burning wood drops upon them from the sky in a shower of sparks. They trample each other in their haste to be gone from this accursed place. They scream and curse me, calling me a madman, hollering for my arrest. I stand untouched where the bonfire stood and holler back.

"You wanted fireworks – I have given them to you! Why do you not *thank* me? Ingrates! Fools!"

Well, the deed is done, my friend, and I am done with this little town. I am revenged and shall tread this earth no more. They will remember Guido Fawkes. Not with joy but with sorrow . . .

"Remember, remember
The fifth of November.
Gunpowder, treason and plot . . .
There is no reason
Why gunpowder treason
Should ever be forgot."

ADVICE FROM
A STRANGER

Advice From a Stranger

I was walking along the road, kicking an empty Coke tin. Mum hated me doing that and that's why I did it. To annoy her. Even though she wasn't there to see me doing it. I knew that if she had been there she would have been annoyed.

I was on my way to school and walking as slowly as I could, hoping I'd be late. I had already missed the morning, but Mum was determined I would be there for half a day. She's like that. Just because I haven't got a dad she tries to boss me around the way he would boss me if I had got one. If you see what I mean.

At least I *have* got a dad, but he pushed off three years ago and, anyway, I didn't care. I still don't care. Good riddance to bad rubbish!

The man was sitting on a low wall at the bottom end of Elderslow Avenue. He was slouching down and his legs were sticking out across the pavement, so I pretended to trip over them and then I said, "You should keep your feet to yourself!" I said it as nastily as I could.

He looked up slowly and stared straight into

111

my face and said, "You took your time. I thought you weren't coming."

He could have been some kind of a tramp by his hair. It was all straggly and needed a wash. He had a bit of a beard, but rather more as though he hadn't bothered to shave. He had blue eyes and one eye, the left one, had a bit of brown mixed in with the blue. His clothes weren't tattered or anything so perhaps he wasn't a real tramp. There was something strange about his clothes, but I couldn't work out what it was. Maybe they didn't fit him properly or something.

He kept staring at me and I said, "Think you'll remember me next time we meet?"

I heard someone say that on the telly once.

He shook his head but didn't answer.

He said, "You'd best get along to school," so I said, "What's it to you?"

He sat up a bit straighter and said, "You should get an education. Believe me, it will make all the difference."

Some kind of nutter, I thought, and I was tempted to say, "Mind your own business!" but he was giving me such a funny look.

Suddenly he said, "You think the whole world's against you, don't you? Well, it isn't."

I was a bit surprised because I *knew* the whole world was against me. Including my mum and dad and all the teachers. I didn't answer and he went on staring at me. Then he said, "Oh Jimmy!"

And that did give me a turn because that's my name and how did he know? He said it very sadly as though it was some kind of big deal.

I said, "Since you know my name you should tell me yours!" I thought that would shake him up a bit. After all, I wasn't going to let anyone push me around, and certainly not some crazy stranger.

He said, "My mates call me Jimbo."

"What mates?" I said it as rudely as I could because there was something odd about him apart from his clothes.

"Never mind what mates!" He shook his head again and said, "They're not all against you. And you should go to school more."

"What's it to you what I do?"

"I can't explain."

I said, "The world's full of nosey parkers!" but he didn't seem to mind. I went on. "Everybody hates me and I hate them back! If I don't want to go to school I stay away."

"I know you do," he said and he sighed. As though he really cared.

I started to get suspicious then. How did he know so much about me? Had my dad sent him to spy on me? For a moment I rather hoped he had, but then I knew he hadn't. Because he didn't care about me.

"I'm nearly old enough to pack in school," I told him.

"Come off it! You're only twelve."

I looked more like fourteen because I was taller than most of the boys in my class. And smarter. They were a bunch of twits. "I'm thirteen and a half!" I lied.

"You're twelve and two months and you think you're tough but you're not."

I felt like punching him right on the nose, but he was a tall man, even sitting down.

A woman came along with a nasty little dog on a lead and we both watched her as she went past. She looked at me with her nose in the air. Stuck-up pig! I stuck my tongue out and wiggled my fingers on the end of nose.

Jimbo said "Stop that!" and gave my hand a slap. A bit half-hearted, but it made me mad.

I kicked him hard on the shin and then I ran down the street as fast as I could. I heard him call out, "Go to school!" so I deliberately went in the other direction.

I turned into Harpington Road and there he was! Waiting for me! He was standing by one of the street lights and his hands were stuffed into his pockets. It was a bit of a shock. How could he have got there?

He said, "Please, Jimmy. Give the world a chance. Go to school and listen to your mother. You won't regret it."

I said, "Is that what you did? Did you go to school?"

He shook his head. "Listen, Jimmy. Do you know where I've been for most of my life? I'll tell you. In jug. In clink. Behind bars."

I tried to think of something flip to say but I couldn't think of anything.

He said, "The first time the magistrate said I'd been led astray and he blamed the other boy because he was older than me. His name was Harris. Douggy Harris. That was nearly forty years ago. The biggest mistake of my life was getting friendly with Douggy Harris. It was the beginning of the end."

We had started walking along the road together and he was telling me about what a mess he'd made of his life. I didn't care about him or his stupid life story but it was better than school.

Then we met Mrs Dann. She's a friend of my mother.

She gave me one of her looks and said to me, "Shouldn't you be at school?"

"It's half term." I looked very innocent. I'm good at telling lies. She looked as though she half believed me and walked past us.

"She'll tell Mum and I'll get a rocket for talking to strangers," I told him.

"No," he said. "She won't say anything about me. You'll see."

It was all right for him to talk. He wouldn't be getting an earful. I would.

"Listen!" he said and his voice was all funny. He grabbed my arm and said, "Please, Jimmy. Remember what I said. The world's a decent place if you give it half a chance. You're a bright lad. Use this!" He tapped his head and smiled. Suddenly I had the strangest feeling that I knew him. I smiled back although I didn't mean to. I don't make a habit of smiling at people. But he had said I was bright. Then he disappeared. No, really. He did. He disappeared. One minute he was there and then he wasn't. Oh yes. I know I tell lies but this is the truth. I felt so peculiar that I went home and Mrs Dann was there. Mum said "Are you feeling OK, love? Mrs Dann thinks you look a bit peaky."

Mrs Dann smiled at me. So she hadn't said anything about Jimbo. Perhaps she wasn't so bad after all.

I shrugged and Mum said, "Early night, Jim. You do look a bit pale."

I smiled at both of them. Why not?

Mum said, "There's new people moving in next door. The son's a bit older than you but he looks a nice enough lad. Their name's Harris."

Harris. The name rang a bell. I took a couple of biscuits out of the packet and went into the garden. There was a boy in the next garden. He had ginger hair and freckles. He said his name was Douglas but I could call him Douggy.

I felt so cold when he said that. I could hardly speak when he asked my name.

"Jimmy?" he said. "Well, I shall call you Jimbo!"

I couldn't answer him. I was shivering with the cold. My teeth were chattering and my stomach felt like ice. He didn't seem to notice. I backed away, mumbling something. You see, I had this idea. This really stupid idea. I ran indoors and up to my room and stared in the mirror. My eyes are blue. I had never noticed before that there was a bit of brown in the left one.

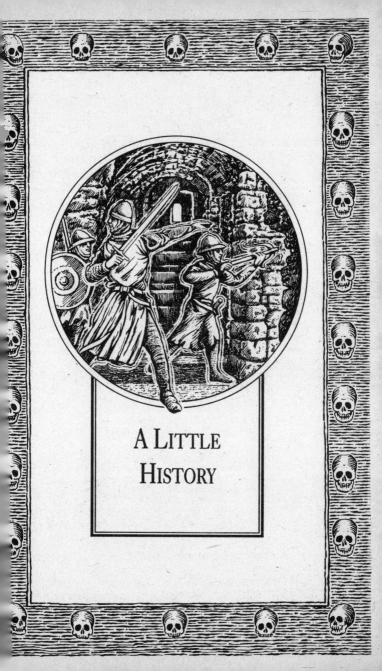

A LITTLE
HISTORY

A Little History

They came across it quite by accident. They turned a bend in the narrow road and there it was, spread out before them like an illustration in a book.

It was a massive fortress built of warm red stone, and its turreted walls almost glowed in the bright sunshine. Don sat up at once and nudged his sister, Claire, who was trying unsuccessfully to fill in a crossword puzzle.

"Can we stop?" they cried together and to their relief their father nodded.

Five minutes later they climbed out of the car, stretched their legs and stared round at the barren, inhospitable landscape.

Mum said, "What a peaceful spot!"

Don said, "It's huge!"

Dad, who was inclined to be informative at the slightest provocation, surveyed the fortress. "Probably fourteenth century – maybe earlier," he said. "Built large enough to sustain a whole village in times of war. The French certainly knew how to build."

As they made their way across the wide drawbridge Don became aware of the silence. "Are we the only tourists here?" he asked.

"Visitors!" said Dad. "We're visitors, not tourists. Tourists are people who drop litter and carry transistors. Visitors are people who truly want to learn something about a foreign country."

Even Mum rolled her eyes at this familiar homily, and Don groaned.

"Well, it's a fact!" Dad insisted.

Inside the fortress, an elderly lady was selling tickets and a small group of people waited nearby with a uniformed guide. Five minutes later they set off on the tour of the fortress. At the first stop the guide spoke in rapid French and the rest of the group nodded with interest.

Dad stepped forward and smiled at the guide. *"Pardon, monsieur, mais nous sommes Anglais,"* he explained. *"Parlez-vous plus lentement, s'il vous plait."*

The rest of the group immediately stared at the foreigners with undisguised interest, but the guide shook his head firmly.

"Je ne comprends pas," he said, and continued his explanation just as quickly as before.

Dad said, "He says he doesn't understand."

"Never mind," said Mum. "We'll just have to concentrate. We might pick up the gist of it."

Don and Claire trailed dutifully along behind the rest while their father did his best to translate the guide's words. "This is where the commanders ate," he whispered. "At least I think so. A sort of officers' mess."

In another room he showed his understanding of the guide's explanation by putting his hands to his head and miming sleep.

The group nodded eagerly, glad to see that the English could appreciate their fortress.

"A dormitory," Dad told Don and Claire.

At the first opportunity Don and Claire dropped back.

"I'd rather wander round on my own," said Don, and Claire agreed.

They heard Dad call, "Hurry up, you two!" but they remained out of sight.

The rest of the footsteps died away. All was quiet.

They looked at each other in triumph.

"Now we can really explore," cried Don, and they went up the first flight of steps they found.

As they mounted the worn stone steps Claire said, "It's strange to think of all the soldiers who came up and down these very stairs. All dead now."

"Dead and forgotten," her brother agreed. "But once they were rushing around here in their chain mail or whatever they wore. Leather breastplates, maybe . . . . Let's go right to the top."

Together they went up a flight of spiralling steps and through a heavy wooden door and found themselves on the roof. They gasped, surprised by the sudden light after the gloom of the steps. They were on some kind of a walkway.

"I suppose the lookouts patrolled round and round the top of the walls," Claire suggested.

They stared out, awed by the vastness of the surrounding plain. The midsummer sun had bleached the grass a dull brown, and the stunted trees cast dark shadows across it. Here and there a large boulder cast further shade. The air was very still and Claire was aware of an almost repressive silence. The birds were silent and the distant tolling of a bell had stopped. She shivered suddenly and her brother looked at her in astonishment.

"You can't be cold!" he exclaimed. "It's baking hot."

"I know," she said slowly, "but I am."

At that moment a small cloud passed in front of the sun and the brightness gave way to a darker haze. Below them, a horse neighed, and then another.

"Horses!" Claire said quickly. She was glad of anything to take her mind off the eerie feeling that something bad was about to happen. She felt threatened without understanding why. Don leaned over to see the horses but there was no sign of them.

Now they could distinctly hear the unmistakable jingle of horses' harness.

"They're down there somewhere," said Don. "Dozens of them."

"Hundreds!" said Claire and suddenly she was trembling all over. "Let's go back to the others," she suggested, but Don wasn't listening.

"I suppose from here they could pour hot oil over the enemy soldiers," he said cheerfully.

"Those horses," said Claire. "Where *are* they?"

Don shrugged and then a loud trumpet blast made them both jump.

"What was that?" cried Claire fearfully.

"A trumpet."

"I know it was a trumpet, stupid! I mean, who blew it?"

Don looked thoughtful. "I bet it's that 'son et lumière'. Like the stuff we saw in Greece last year. You remember. They had bits of the Parthenon all lit up and they played tapes of music and voices and – sounds."

"I hope so," said Claire. "Don – I'm scared!"

Before he could assure her that there was nothing to be frightened of, the door through which they had reached the roof was suddenly thrust wide open and somebody – or some thing

– rushed past them, bumping into Claire and almost knocking her over.

But they saw no one.

"Oh Don!" Claire whispered. "I didn't imagine that, did I? Oh! What's happening?"

All around them voices shouted orders in rapid French and they were aware of an excitement in the air. As they clung together, invisible footsteps hurried to and fro; someone fell over them and they heard him cursing as he scrambled to his feet.

Claire's heart seemed to have stopped beating and a glance at her brother's face showed her that he, too, knew what was going on.

"It's the soldiers! They're getting ready for battle!" Don hissed. "I mean, the ghosts of the soldiers. They must be ghosts, mustn't they?"

"I don't know. I don't want to know!" she told him shakily.

Down below they could hear hundreds of men moving about, and the air was electric. The attacking army was preparing to batter its way into the fortress. The defenders were preparing to repel them. All was confusion and noise.

A new sound presented itself. The sound of heavy wheeled machinery approached the walls of the fortress, creaking and groaning as it was manhandled into place. There was a crash to their left and several men screamed out in pain.

"What was that?" cried Claire, but she covered her ears and did not hear Don's answer that it might be a cannon ball.

"We've got to get away from here," he told his sister but his commonsense told him that their chances of reaching the stairs was slight. But if they stayed on the roof they might be killed.

Could someone be killed by a phantom cannon ball? Don didn't want to find out!

The battle raged around them. They identified the hum of arrows and the clash of steel. They heard scaling ladders being propped against the wall – and screams from those on it as it was pushed away. They saw nothing at all, except in their imaginations, though that was enough. The sounds and smells – of sweat, blood and fear – were more than they could bear. Suddenly a man close beside them screamed out in agony and fell across them, winding them both with his weight.

"That's it!" shouted Don. "We've got to make a run for it!" Without waiting for his sister's reply, he wriggled out from beneath the soldier's body and dragged Claire after him.

"He might be dead!" she cried – but what could they do if he were? There was no time to waste on speculation.

Together they pushed their way towards the door and finally made it. Getting down took further time. So many other people were using the stairs. It seemed an eternity before they were once more safely at the bottom.

They paused to stare grimly at one another.

Claire said, "It's not quite so loud down here."

"You're right. It's fading."

They ran along a corridor, relieved to discover that the sound of battle was definitely receding.

It took them quite a while to find the rest of the party, but by the time they did they had left the battle behind them.

Their father looked up, annoyed with them.

"Where have you two been?" he demanded.

Mum said "You look a bit odd. What have you been up to?"

"Nothing!" they chorused but now the guide shushed them, anxious to reach the end of his account.

Dad looked at them suspiciously and Claire had to admit that they did look a little dishevelled. Don's face was still pale, and she guessed her own was too.

"Well, pay attention now you're here," said Dad sternly. "This guide's very good. You might just learn a little history."

THE MIRACLE

The Miracle

The audition was at three o'clock. Tim glanced at his watch and began to hurry. Not that he was feeling very hopeful but his mother had insisted that he apply for the part. Tim was slim and good-looking in a classic way. His mother always described him as 'the Greek God' type, which made him squirm with embarrassment.

His mother had wanted passionately to go on the stage, but had shown no talent for acting whatsoever. She had found it impossible to learn lines and had also been blessed with 'two left feet'! So she could not become a dancer, either, which had been a great trial to her. To compensate for this disappointment she had decided that Tim, her only child, should become a famous actor in her stead. At the age of three he had started dancing classes with Miss Brands and now, at the age of twelve, had been enrolled at a stage school. His mother had hinted that when funds allowed he would have singing lessons – a prospect which filled him with dread.

Tim had grown up with the knowledge that he was destined for the stage and, although he loathed the idea, he was reluctant to break his mother's heart by telling her that he wanted to be an accountant. Tim had a way with figures and money fascinated him. His teachers had tried to persuade his mother to let him stay on at school to take his maths exams. Unsuccessfully, of course. Tim had known right from the start that it was hopeless. His mother's mind was made up, and only a miracle would change it.

With a sigh he presented himself at the stage door of the run-down theatre where the auditions were to be held. It was what his mother called 'a nice little role' with a few lines and rather more dancing. Tim felt sure he could get the part. He had a good speaking voice and he could dance. The problem was that he hated it all.

The door was closed and so he rang the bell, banged on the door with his knuckles and then rang the bell again. There was no answer. He wondered if he dared go home, but his courage failed him. Normally, of course, his mother accompanied him on all these trips. Today, however, she was suffering from flu, and had sent him on his own.

Tim wandered round to the side of the building, looking for another entrance. He found a small emergency exit that was open and, with a deep sigh, he made his way inside.

To his surprise the huge auditorium was empty. Silence surrounded him as he stared round at the vast interior of the theatre which looked eerie in the dim light provided by the EXIT signs.

"Must be early," he said aloud, and his voice echoed in the gloom.

"Must have got the time wrong," he said, a little louder.

It was a strange feeling to be the only person in the auditorium, and the sound of his own voice was somehow reassuring.

He wandered up the aisle between the rows of empty seats and stopped at row H. Turning towards the stage he declared in a loud voice, "I am the ghost of Banquo!" and added a horrible, spooky laugh.

Suddenly an idea occurred to him. Why shouldn't he go on stage and get the feel of it? There was no one to say 'No', so he hurried towards the stage. Between Tim and the stage, however, there was a barrier in the shape of the orchestra pit. This was a space where the orchestra sat with their instruments to play the music that accompanied the play.

With some difficulty Tim climbed down into the pit and from there he reached the stage.

At last he was standing in the centre of the large stage, looking out over the rows of empty seats.

He struck a dramatic pose and cried "Friends, Romans, countrymen! Lend me your ears!" and then began to giggle. Grinning, he cried "Mum! Look at me! I'm on the West End stage!" He did a few steps of one of the dances Miss Brands had taught him recently and laughed at the staccato sound his shoes made on the bare boards.

He stopped abruptly. Surely he could hear soft footfalls! Someone was coming. He began to panic. He shouldn't be on the stage without permission, but he didn't want to be seen climbing back through the orchestra pit.

Tim stared into the darkness and suddenly he saw a vague figure sitting in the fourth row. It was a man with long hair, dressed in a dark jacket and frilled shirt. He was also wearing some kind of hat. A bit overdressed, thought Tim, but said nothing. Probably David Jennings, the casting director.

"Well!" boomed the man. "Get on with it, lad!"

It was a very loud voice for such an insubstantial figure!

Tim said "Er – what shall I do?"

"D'you dance?"

"Yes."

"Well, we've no pianist so that's no good."

"Oh! No, I suppose not."

Tim supposed he was the casting director. It was his job to choose the six successful applicants who would be given parts in the play.

"D'you sing, lad?" he boomed again.

"Yes but —"

"I know! We've got no pianist!"

He roared with laughter and Tim smiled weakly. He wondered where the others were. There should be dozens of boys auditioning, as well as a secretary to take down the casting director's notes.

The man stood up and moved into the aisle between the seats, and Tim saw with surprise that he was wearing knee breeches. Probably getting into the feel of the play, he thought.

"So you want to be an actor, eh?"

There was something strange about him, but Tim couldn't put his finger on it. His clothes were so dark that he seemed almost invisible.

Tim opened his mouth to say 'Yes, sir' but the words stuck in his throat.

"Well, do you or don't you?" The man's eyes glittered and Tim felt a shiver of unease.

Again he found it hard to answer and only managed a croak.

"It's a hard life," said the director. "More kicks than halfpennies! But if it's in your blood . . . . If!"

Tim had the uncomfortable feeling that Mr Jennings could see into his heart, could read his innermost secrets. He sensed the disapproval on the man's face and felt that he saw him as the imposter he really was.

"My mother—" he began.

The director settled himself in the front row and stretched his legs comfortably. "Well, lad," he said crossly, "I haven't got all day! If you're going to show me what you can do, you'd best make a start. Entertain me! Make me laugh!"

Tim's heart sank. He did know a few jokes but they had immediately deserted him.

"I'm sorry –" he stammered. "I'll say a speech. Er—" He searched his mind desperately. All that came to mind were a few lines from one of Shakespeare's plays.

Raising his voice he began in ringing tones:

> "The quality of mercy is not strain'd,
>   It droppeth as the gentle rain from heaven
>   Upon the—"

The director interrupted him brusquely. "Not that again! I've heard Portia's speech more times than I can count on fingers and toes. Try something else, damn you!"

Tim hid his resentment at the director's rudeness and tried frantically to think of something else.

A few lines from *Macbeth* presented themselves.

"Methought I heard a voice cry, 'Sleep no more!

Macbeth does murder sleep.' "

Tim thought he had done it rather well and looked down hopefully towards the director. Mr Jennings was nowhere to be seen.

"Mr Jennings?" called Tim.

A footstep behind him made him jump and, as he turned, he was astonished to see the casting director hurrying towards him from the back of the stage. There was a wild expression in his eyes and he was muttering a string of curses.

Before Tim could even think of running the man had reached him and was reaching out with trembling hands for the lapels of Tim's blazer.

"You stupid, ignorant puppy!" he whispered through clenched teeth. He shook Tim violently, ignoring his efforts to wriggle free. "You dared to say that word in my hearing! You snivelling little—"

"W-what word?" cried Tim, somehow managing to free himself from the man's clutches. It was just his luck, he thought, that on the one occasion when his mother would have been useful she was at home in bed with flu.

"*That* word!" cried his tormentor. "The word all real actors never say. The word that calls down the wrath of all things evil. The word that brought about my downfall!"

Tim looked round desperately for a way of escape, but the wings of the stage were in darkness and he didn't think he stood much chance of finding his way out. He would have to go back the way he had come – across the orchestra pit. Tentatively he took a step backwards, but at once the director stepped forward so that there was less than a foot between them.

Tim saw with a prickle of fear that the man's mouth was flecked with foam and his eyes were bloodshot. He took another step backwards but the man's arm shot out and grabbed him once more.

"They pelted me, lad! What d'you think of that? Pelted me! Hounded me! Drove me to despair!" He lowered his voice dramatically. "To the point of insanity. And all because I said that word." Suddenly he raised his voice and roared "MACBETH! MACBETH! Oh yes! He'll murder sleep! No doubt of that!" He released Tim suddenly and his expression changed. "They hated me. They were jealous. I had talent and they were as wooden as an oak tree! One night I could bear it no more. I drank a pint or two of ale and then another and another. Then I went home to my garret and—" He clutched his throat with a gesture that struck terror into Tim's heart.

"That's right, lad! I hanged meself!"

Tim's thoughts whirled crazily. If this man was telling the truth then he was dead!

"But—" he stammered hoarsely "but you're here – I mean, how could you—"

The man narrowed his eyes, but not before Tim had recognised the hatred in them. Several things became horribly clear to him. This was not the casting director. This was a madman, or worse, and he meant to do Tim harm. His instinct was to turn and run, but before he could do so the man lunged forward and pushed him violently and Tim felt himself falling into the blackness of the deserted pit.

He struck his head on something hard and the last thing he remembered was the man glaring down at him from the edge of the stage.

Tim was discovered nearly two hours later by David Jennings when he turned up for the audition. Tim's leg was broken in two places and he was unconscious. A week later he was still in hospital with his leg in plaster. The consultant broke the news to him reluctantly. Tim had been very lucky, he said. It was a very nasty fracture but they had saved his leg. It would be a slow job but it would heal eventually. He would always have a limp, the consultant told him, and he would never make a footballer. Apart from that, there was nothing to worry about.

Tim almost laughed aloud, but he didn't, because the consultant was taking it all so seriously. Tim wasn't worried. He was delighted. Who had ever heard of a Greek god with one leg shorter than the other? How could he be a famous actor or a dancer with a limp? Not even his mother could argue with that. It was the perfect excuse. Now, thanks to whoever *or whatever* he had seen at the theatre, he could dabble in pounds and pence for the rest of his life. He could be an accountant.

He watched his mother tripping cheerfully along the ward between the beds and his face broke into a broad grin. "Mum," he said, as soon as she had settled herself on a chair. "I've got something to tell you . . ."

AMNESIA

Amnesia

Judy sat up in bed and hugged her knees with a growing feeling of panic. She stared round the bedroom with frightened eyes as the dreadful truth dawned on her. The people in the room with her were perfect strangers to her. Or if they were not then she had no recollection of them at all. If they were people she knew, then she had somehow forgotten them.

There was a tall man with a dark moustache – the sort that Mexican bandits wore. But he was too pale to be Mexican. She had seen his eyes and they were grey like her own. Could he be her father? She could see no other resemblance between them but she might take after her mother.

The man was standing by the window, staring down.

He said, "It's a nice big garden. A bit overgrown, but we could make something of it. What d'you think, Nancy?"

He had an American accent! So he could not be her father unless she too had an American accent. She couldn't remember whether she had or not.

She glanced at the two women to see which one answered. The younger woman moved to the window and said "It's OK, but – oh heck! I'm not happy about the idea."

The older woman remained sitting on the stool in front of the dressing table. Judy wondered if she might be her grandmother. Was she Nancy's mother? And was Nancy her own mother?

The panic grew within her but she tried to reason with herself. She must have been ill and she had lost her memory. There was a word for that, but she couldn't remember it. Soon she would get better and everything would become clear again. In the meantime she didn't want to reveal how little she understood. She would wait. If the man put his arm round her and hugged her – well, he was probably her father. In a moment one of them would speak to her and that might give her a clue to her identity. If only she could recall her own name!

Nancy was tall with very dark hair, whereas Judy's was red and curly. Perhaps they were an aunt and uncle! On a visit to see how she was recovering from her illness. That made sense, she told herself eagerly. She began to wonder how she had become ill and – amnesia! That was the word! Total memory loss. She felt slightly cheered. Her memory was obviously coming back, but how had she lost it? A bang on the head or a road accident, maybe? A brain infection? She was rather vague about the latter. Or maybe she had suffered a shock. Shock could play nasty tricks on people's minds.

Glancing at the others to make sure she was unobserved, she pulled up the hem of her nightdress but could see no signs of bruising, no scars, no bandages. And she felt fine. She pulled the nightdress down to cover her legs again.

The old lady said, "I liked the kitchen, George, and it's already been modernized. Oh do think about it, Nancy. It's such a bargain."

Nancy said "It's only a bargain because—"

And the man, George, said, "Oh for Pete's sake! Don't keep bringing that up! We knew all that when we decided to see the place."

Nancy half turned and her expression was worried. "I get the feeling, in here particularly, that we're being watched."

"Oh, don't be ridiculous!" he snapped. "The price is right, the location is right – not ten minutes walk from the office—"

The old lady said quickly, "But suppose we are being watched? She was only a child. A child wouldn't be malevolent, would she?"

They had turned away from the window but none of them glanced in Judy's direction. She had changed her mind about them. They weren't her parents. They were people who were thinking of buying the house. Presumably they felt a bit awkward looking at the bedroom with a girl ill in bed.

Judy said, "I don't mind. Really."

Her voice sounded so weak! She must have been ill a long time. Maybe she had been in a coma.

Obviously none of them heard her, for they didn't answer.

Probably at any moment her mother or father would come into the room to speak to them.

A coma. She didn't like that idea. Sometimes people in comas finally came to and had forgotten how to speak or eat or walk. Hastily she imagined herself sitting at a table managing a knife and fork and relief flooded through her. She had not forgotten everything.

Nancy said, "Don't you feel a presence here? In this room? And she fell from this very window! It's such a terrible thought. I can't get it out of my mind."

George said, "Yes, dear, but it was years ago. You really shouldn't let it get to you this way. It's not like you to be so unreasonable."

Judy frowned. Had *she* fallen from the window, and is that how she had got the amnesia? But if that was years ago she ought to be older. She still felt like a child, and the nightdress was printed with sprigs of flowers and had a pocket. And her long red hair was tied in two bunches. A new wave of panic swept through her and without knowing why she called out, "Who am I? Oh, please tell me!"

Nancy turned towards her and said sharply, "I heard something! A voice. You must have heard it!"

George and the old lady shook their heads.

George said, "It's that imagination of yours!"

"No!" Nancy insisted. "I heard a voice. Very faint but – oh, don't look at me that way! I tell you I heard someone."

George looked at the old lady and shrugged. "Well, Mother, I guess that settles it. This house gets the 'thumbs down'! We'll go and look at the other property after lunch."

Mother and son left the room but Nancy lingered. She looked fearfully around and whispered, "I know you're there. I know you mean us no harm but – oh what the heck am I doing? Talking to a ghost!"

Judy scrambled towards the end of the bed and cried out, "Don't go! Please don't go!"

But Nancy pulled the door to behind her and Judy heard their footsteps on the stairs.

She ran to the door and tried to open it but her strength was waning fast.

She ran to the window and saw them below on the path, walking towards the gate, towards

147

the waiting car that was parked outside. Judy was gripped by a terrible loneliness. "Wait!" she screamed, but her scream was soundless. She leaned through the window, calling them back – and leaned just a little too far. She began to fall and went on falling through eternity.

And only then did she remember that she was already dead.

Nancy Drew
Mystery Stories

Nancy Drew is the best-known and most-loved girl detective ever. Join her and her best friends, George Fayne and Bess Marvin, in her many thrilling adventures available in Armada.

Armada

The Chalet School
Series
ELINOR M. BRENT-DYER

Elinor M. Brent-Dyer has written many books about life at the famous alpine school. Follow the thrilling adventures of Joey, Mary-Lou and all the other well-loved characters in these delightful stories, available only in Armada.

Chalet School Three-in-One (containing The Chalet School in Exile, The Chalet School at War, and The Highland Twins at the Chalet School)   £4.99

Armada

The Three Investigators Mysteries

Meet the Three Investigators – brilliant Jupiter Jones, athletic Pete Crenshaw and studious Bob Andrews. Their motto, "We investigate anything" has led them into some bizarre and dangerous situations. Join the three boys in their sensational mysteries, available only in Armada.

Armada

Have you read all the adventures in the "Mystery" series by Enid Blyton? Here are some of them:

The Rockingdown Mystery

Roger, Diana, Snubby and Barney hear strange noises in the cellar while staying at Rockingdown Hall. Barney goes to investigate and makes a startling discovery . . .

The Rilloby Fair Mystery

Valuable papers have disappeared – the Green Hands Gang has struck again! Which of Barney's workmates at the circus is responsible? The four friends turn detectives – and have to tackle a dangerous criminal.

The Ring o' Bells Mystery

Eerie things happen at deserted Ring o' Bells Hall – bells start to ring, strange noises are heard in a secret passage, and there are some very unfriendly strangers about. Something very mysterious is going on, and the friends mean to find out what.

The Rockingdown Mystery	£2.75
The Rilloby Fair Mystery	£2.75
The Ring o' Bells Mystery	£2.75

Armada

Have you seen
the Hardy Boys
lately?

Now you can continue to enjoy the Hardy Boys in a new action-packed series written especially for older readers. Each book has more high-tech adventure, intrigue, mystery and danger than ever before.

Join Frank and Joe in these fabulous adventures, available only in Armada.

1	Dead on Target	£2.75	☐
2	Evil, Incorporated	£2.75	☐
3	Cult of Crime	£2.75	☐
4	The Lazarus Plot	£2.75	☐
5	Edge of Destruction	£2.75	☐
6	The Crowning Terror	£2.75	☐
7	Deathgame	£2.75	☐
8	See No Evil	£2.75	☐
9	Genius Thieves	£2.75	☐
10	Hostages of Hate	£2.75	☐

Armada

The Pit

ANN CHEETHAM

The summer has hardly begun when Oliver Wright is plunged into a terrifying darkness. Gripped by fear when workman Ted Hoskins is reduced to a quivering child at a demolition site, Oliver believes something of immense power has been disturbed. But what?

Caught between two worlds – the confused present and the tragic past – Oliver is forced to let events take over.

£2.50 ☐

Nightmare Park

LINDA HOY

A highly original and atmospheric thriller set around a huge modern theme park, a theme park where teenagers suddenly start to disappear . . .

£2.50 ☐

Armada

All these books are available at your local bookshop or newsagent, or can be ordered from the publisher. To order direct from the publishers just tick the title you want and fill in the form below:

Name _____

Address _____

_____

Send to: Collins Childrens Cash Sales
           PO Box 11
           Falmouth
           Cornwall
           TR10 9EN

Please enclose a cheque or postal order or debit my Visa/ Access –

  Credit card no:

  Expiry date:

  Signature:

– to the value of the cover price plus:

UK and BFPO: £1 for the first book and 20p per copy for each additional book ordered.

Overseas and Eire: £2.95 service charge.

Armada reserve the right to show new retail prices on covers which may differ from those previously advertised in the text or elswhere.

Armada